50p

FIGG

FIGGETTY POODEN

The dialect verse of
EDWARD SLOW

Selected and introduced by
John Chandler

TROWBRIDGE
WILTSHIRE LIBRARY & MUSEUM SERVICE
1982

PUBLISHED BY WILTSHIRE LIBRARY & MUSEUM SERVICE
BYTHESEA ROAD, TROWBRIDGE, WILTSHIRE
DIRECTOR: C. W. FRANKLIN, FLA

DESIGNED BY EDWARD J. KELLY, ALA
PRINTED BY SWINDON PRESS LTD., ELGIN DRIVE, SWINDON
ISBN 0 86080 095 4

Contents

Acknowledgments

Wiltshire Library & Museum Service wishes to thank: Miss Rosemary Olivier, for giving permission to reproduce an extract from *Without knowing Mr. Walkley*, by Edith Olivier; Wilton Historical Society, for giving permission to reproduce the photograph of Edward Slow from an original in the Society's custody; Wiltshire Archaeological and Natural History Society, for allowing access to Slow items in the Society's library; Wiltshire Record Office, for allowing access to Wilton parish records.

Who was Edward Slow?

Mention the name Edward Slow to an old Wiltshireman and the chances are that memories will stir of the legend of the moonrakers as recited at countless social gatherings throughout Wiltshire in the early years of this century. Indeed, my own copy of his collected rhymes, inscribed on the flyleaf, "Burbage Women's Institute March 1923", was doubtless originally purchased for just such a purpose. Slow was an old man when today's octogenarians were children, and it is hardly surprising that his work came to be regarded after his death as quaint and old-fashioned. All his publications have been out of print for many years, and second-hand copies of even his most popular book, his collected rhymes, are regarded as scarce. Some of his more ephemeral pamphlets must by now be extremely rare. This is a great pity. The language and society which Slow recorded and of which he was a part have now receded from our memory; I am sure that I am not the only west-countryman never to have heard the word "girt" used in earnest. His work is now the more valuable, not only for its dialect and its entertainment, but also as a chronicle of the way in which rural Wiltshire moved from the nineteenth to the twentieth century, by one fervent Wiltshireman who took a keen interest in everything around him.

Edward Slow was born at Wilton in 1841, and seems to have been the youngest to survive of a large family. His father, whose forebears had originated in Huntingdon, died during the cholera epidemic in 1849, when Edward was seven, and the family found themselves in financial difficulties. By 1851 two of his older sisters were working in the carpet factory at Wilton, and a brother was employed as an errand boy. Hannah Slow, the widowed mother, continued to live at Wilton, where in earlier years she had trained silk-weavers, until her eventual death in 1898 at the grand age of ninety. It was probably from her that Edward learnt the art of story-telling and his love of the past. The young Edward was sent to Wilton Free School for five years, where he apparently acquired "the three Wiltshire R's and the rudiments of learning", which he supplemented by whatever reading matter he could find at the Literary Institute. At the age of fourteen he was apprenticed to a wheelwright and coachbuilder in Salisbury, and seems to have made a good impression on his master. On completing his apprenticeship he returned to Wilton and set up in business on his own, renting a workshop at Ditchampton with a half-sovereign given him by his master. In the early years of his carriage-building career he seems to have been in partnership with a Mr. Stone, but by 1875 he was advertising himself as, "Edward Slow, coach builder and wheelwright, spring van, trap and waggon builder". His business seems to have prospered, so that by the late 1890s he was able to offer it for sale (it was bought by F. W. Marks, whose firm is still trading at Ditchampton as motor engineers) and embark on a long and comfortable retirement in the house he had built for himself, "Ellandune" in Ditchampton (now 54, Shaftesbury Road), with the wife whom he had married in 1865 and with whom he would celebrate their diamond wedding anniversary shortly before his death, on 16th February 1925.

Slow's rise from the obscurity of a pauper orphan to a successful Wilton businessman was accompanied by an almost chauvinistic pride in his native town. It was partly through his efforts that Wilton was granted a new borough charter in 1885, and he served on the newly-constituted Borough Council, with one short break, until shortly before his death. He was elected Mayor of Wilton in 1892 and for a second term in 1905; from 1893, when the honour was accorded him, he was regularly known in Wilton as "Alderman Slow''. His public life included other worthy causes, which he served as committee member or trustee, and he was also interested in church affairs and Conservative politics. By the 1920s as he grew old in his cottage, surrounded by his stamp collection and his library, he had become very much of an establishment figure, the last of ''the old school'', with a long white beard concealing the fact that he wore no collar and tie. Perhaps because he had outlived most of his contemporaries his passing, when it came, seems not to have been greatly mourned in his home town. He was not forgotten, however, and his flamboyant character made an impression on one young resident of Wilton, Edith Olivier, a better writer than he, who vividly recorded her memories of him some years later:

> Wilton then had its poet, Edward Slow, the carriage-builder, a man of rugged face and figure, and with a loud resonant voice which sounded all down the street when he met a friend for a quiet talk. He was a master of the old Wiltshire speech, and his rhymes were not merely written in the dialect, but they came up directly from the dialect mind. He was an entirely descriptive writer, and he described what fell under his own eyes. Slow was no visionary. He was a racy and realistic observer, and his subjects were those things which outstand in the memory of the untravelled countrymen—public dinners, fox-hunting, or a visit to London. When country fairs are things of the past, Slow's *Our girt Zeptember Vair* will bring before the mind of future generations, exact and living pictures of the events of every hour in the day of the chief West of England sheep fair in the nineteenth century. But by then, the poem will be written in a dead language, for Slow's was the true Wiltshire dialect, unspoilt by any school-board varnish. He was the last of the old minstrels, for his rhymes really came to life when he read or recited them himself, giving immense delight both to himself and his hearers.

Slow had the countryman's distrust of the foreigner, and some few years before the Great War, he received a letter from a German Philological Society, inviting him to go to London to have gramophone records made from his reading of some of his poems, in order to help these scholars to learn the true pronunciation. Slow was immediately suspicious. He was convinced that the Germans had some ulterior motive, and he refused to answer the letter. Several more came, and at last he silenced these determined correspondents with a post-card on which he wrote in his large deliberate hand-writing: "Mr. Slow does not intend to go to London".

Years afterwards, he read in the *Daily Mail* that the Italian repulse by the Germans had been prepared for by a previous penetration of the villages behind the lines by Germans who had learnt the North Italian patois from gramophone records. He cut this report out of the paper, and carried it for months in his pocket, to show to every one he met, how far-sighted he had been.

Slow believed in a Freemasonry among poets, and thought that they should always be ready to exchange their works one with another. He wrote to Lord Tennyson telling him this, and enclosing a copy of his *Wiltshire Rhymes*, and he was very proud when a copy of the Poet Laureate's poems came in return; and in the train he could always find out when a fellow passenger was a writer, and would get into conversation and arrange an exchange of *Works*.

Slow seems to have discovered his peculiar literary talent by accident. "I began to write when I was 23", he was to tell a reporter in 1911. "There was a harvest home festival at a village near by, and the parson [Rev. Trotman of Burcombe] asked me to do something for it, so I wrote a Harvest Home rhyme in dialect. That took so well that it was printed, and, as it obtained an encouraging sale, I set to work at a book of rhymes in the same strain." Slow's first collection, *Poems in the Wiltshire dialect*, was published in 1867, and came to the attention of a Salisbury printer, Frederick Blake. Blake and Slow became firm friends, and from 1870 until 1892, when Blake died, all Slow's output, which included his best and most popular verse, was published by Blake. After his first volume Slow was inclined not to refer to his work as poetry, but preferred the less pretentious "rhymes". Nevertheless, one of these rhymes, *The Wiltshire moonrakers*, which first appeared one hundred years ago in 1881 (although based on a much older legend), quickly attained the status of a national epic among Wiltshiremen, to be recounted whenever the county's pride was at stake, whenever it was felt necessary to show that, "ther baint no vlies on we".

Most of Slow's dialect verse first appeared in a series of six volumes of Wiltshire rhymes, published at intervals throughout his working life, from 1867 to 1898. With a few exceptions all the pieces in the present volume originally appeared in this way. However, during the 1890s, after Blake's death, and perhaps at the suggestion of his new publisher, R. R. Edwards, his literary endeavours broadened into new fields. He had already placed his interest in dialect on a more serious footing in 1889, when he included a glossary of Wiltshire words in the fourth volume of Wiltshire rhymes. In 1892 an expanded version of the glossary was printed as a separate pamphlet; he also contributed to the work of the English Dialect Society. The fifth volume of rhymes, published in about 1894, included prose pieces for the first time, and these and many others went to make up one of Slow's more substantial volumes, *Humourous west countrie tales*, published in 1899. The tales range from short stories originally published as separate pamphlets, such as *Ben Sloper's visit to the Zalsbury diamond jubilee zelebrayshun* . . . to three-line anecdotes, such as *Counting tha sheep*: "Varmir, ta new sheppherd bwoy, 'Didst count tha sheep las night bwoy?' Bwoy, 'Eece zur, ael bit dree, they kep runnin about zoo, I cooden count em'''. Slow's interest in international affairs and British nationalism—a highly infectious enthusiasm in the late-Victorian and Edwardian years—has also left its mark in a number of short jingoistic pieces of this period, with emotive titles such as *Who's to blame? Boer or Briton . . .* He also began to experiment with dialects other than his own—plantation negro in *The spider and the fly*, of 1903, and cockney in the largest work of his later years, *Jan Ridley's new wife*, 1913. This latter work is interesting, because it marks Slow's last attempt at a different genre, in this case the novel. But it is not really a novel, merely an extended narrative engineered to give its author the maximum opportunity to write dialogues which contrasted the Wiltshire and cockney dialects. But one other work of his retirement years does find the author in a comfortable new role, that of historian. *The chronology of Wilton . . .*, published in 1903, is a serious attempt at historical writing which admirably displays Slow's interest in history, but more especially his love of anything connected with his home town. If ever there was a labour of love it is this; reading it now one can still sense the pride with which he was able to include his own name among the list of mayors, and alongside Lady Herbert as a local author.

Slow's writing after Blake's death in 1892 is not only more varied and, in my opinion, generally less good—his true genre being the dialect rhyme—it is also more complicated from a bibliographical point of view. Many of his dialogues and tales were first published as separate pamphlets, often to coincide with particular events—a circus at Salisbury (*Barnum and Bailey's girtest show on earth*) or *The military manoovers on Zalsbury plaain*—which drew great crowds and therefore offered the publisher a ready sale. But apart from the colour which such works add to our other sources of information about these events only the substantial *Rekerlections an' yarns of a woold Zalsbury carrier . . .* is of real value. Slow intended his last work to be *Jan Ridley's new wife*, the novel, published in 1913, but the great war prompted him to take up his pen for one more patriotic pamphlet. At the time of his death in 1925 Slow's poems were still popular, and his publisher claimed that orders were received from expatriate Wiltshiremen all over the world. In about 1903 the best of his verse had been presented afresh in *The Wiltshire moonraker's edition of west countrie rhymes*, and it is this attractive volume which continued to sell and from which the present selection has been made.

Had Slow been asked what he thought was the value of his little books, he would have replied that they recorded a dialect which was fast disappearing. Like Hardy and many another west-countryman he could see influences at work which would suppress and then eliminate the native patois. By 1881 he was expressing this view: "Tho much it da pain I ta vind that ower poor wold lainguide ater livin za long, is likely zoon ta die out. Wat we Railways, Telegraps, School Bouards &c, &c, I'm aveard till zoon becom a thing a tha pass". He realised, too, that simply writing down the utterances of his own tongue was not enough; he must listen attentively to the anecdotes of his friends and chance acquaintances, recording not only their accents, but the way in which they expressed their thoughts. When preparing his glossary for publication he described his methods: "In my many long rambles I have purposely engaged in conversation with the shepherd on the down, the ploughman in the field, the woodman in the copse, and the general labourer about the farm, in order to glean from their own mouths words in their purest simplicity. On these occassions [*sic*] I invariably used the broadest Wiltshire I am capable of, so that it never once entered their minds or had they the remotest suspicion, 'a chiel was amang them takin notes'. Many a humourous and quaint story have I heard from these rural folk, which I trust, some day may see the light . . ." Slow's dialect, therefore, was not the spurious 'Mummerset' dreamed up by urbane scriptwriters to portray slow-witted country folk, but a genuine attempt to record the sounds of the Wilton countryside a century ago. It does not, of course, have the exactness of the *Survey of English dialects*, which uses the phonetic alphabet and takes pains not to influence the subject's pronunciation, and so it is not precise enough for modern philologists. But that is no criticism of Slow's efforts.

Apart from the dialect in which it is couched, Slow's verse was intended to be enjoyed as simple entertainment, especially when read aloud. No-one would pretend that it is great literature—many plots seem contrived, many rhymes are doggerel, and many jokes fall flat. But that does not matter. Slow had an unquenchable talent to entertain his audience, and two of his themes—the shrewdness of apparently stupid country folk, and the mischievous mocking of an oppressive authority—were calculated always to provoke a sympathetic smile. And once or twice Slow's work does rise above its simple rhyming couplets. *Good Vridy las* is obviously the result of a genuinely cherished experience which the author has worked with some care into an evocative poem. The result is perhaps the most satisfying piece, from a literary point of view, in this selection.

But the passage of time has brought a new value to Slow's work. He recorded the highlights and experiences of Victorian working-class life in a part of Wiltshire which was then relatively unaffected by polite society, and which has now disappeared. Poverty and the struggle to find enough to eat are the themes of many of the pieces in this selection, from the pathos of *Gramfer shaant goo inta wirkhouse*, to *Tha girt vat pig*, which is a beautiful blend of sorrow at the death of a pet mingled with joy at the prospect of the feasts resulting from that death. Others reflect the tasks of the countryside (*Haymeakin zong*), the characters who made their living there (*Smilin Jack*) and poor but loving family life (*Meakin out tha zensus peaper*). But special treatment was reserved for the great occasions which seasoned even the poorest existence, the simple celebrations which Slow so evidently enjoyed, and for which he wrote so many of his rhymes. *Our girt Zeptember vair, Poll's weddin*, and *Gramfer's crismis*, whatever their merits as poetry, may now be regarded as valuable eye-witness accounts of long-forgotten ways of doing things. *Gipsyun at Stounhenge*, too, is a marvellous description of a happy day from Slow's childhood, when the whole family trundled up the Woodford valley in a horse-van for a picnic at Stonehenge.

Of course Slow was not the only writer to have recorded Victorian country life in the Wiltshire countryside. Richard Jefferies and W. H. Hudson were both observers of the scene, and both their descriptions (*Hodge and his masters* and *A shepherd's life*) are now rightly regarded as classics. But Slow, although inferior as a writer, was no mere observer; he was a participant in the things he described. And, unlike most writers of humble origins, he did not try to rise from the ranks of the working classes, or, like Alfred Williams, try to interpret working-class ways to his intellectual friends. Slow was writing for the "leabourin volk", of which he was one, recalling to their minds the pleasures of their society, making light of their hardships with a joke, poking fun at the squire and eulogizing the crafty smuggler. He is seen at his best in *Tha girt harcheology*, where he gently lampoons the Wiltshire Archaeological Society's meeting at Wilton in 1870, accusing the members of being more interested in the food that was provided for them than in the antiquities which they were supposed to be inspecting. His description of the proceedings is amply borne out by the official report in the *Wiltshire archaeological magazine*: "Mr. Motton catered with his usual liberality, but owing to the crowded state of the room ["As thick as any vlees"—Slow], the waiting was not so good as probably it would otherwise have been. Lady

Herbert sent a magnificent buck, and also a large supply of game. The dessert, which was of the best, was also the gift of her ladyship [''Ther thay did stuff an vill away, Unger an thirst ta quench''—Slow]''. And later: ''In a spacious tent erected near the house, a capital cold collation was provided [''Vor everywhere wur thay did goo, Nice veasts wur ael spread out''—Slow] . . . The company then left the tent, and proceeded to Wilton . . . Mr. Swayne invited the party to tea at the Island, and a goodly number of ladies and gentlemen responded to the invitation [''An ael did look za jolly well, An plaz'd as thay could be; Var skierce bit veasten ael that time, Be these Harchaeology.''—Slow]''.

The historian must ever beware lest his picture of the past is coloured by a minority—the goodly ladies and gentlemen who took tea with Mr. Swayne—whose version tends to have survived, whereas the history of the majority—the picnickers at Stonehenge—remains for the large part unwritten. The subjects—in this case food and archaeology—may be the same, but in the attitudes and prejudices there is a world of difference. It fell to Edward Slow to speak for the silent majority, and this little book gives him a chance to make his voice heard again.

John Chandler
July 1981

Sources used in introductory essay

Apart from the works of Edward Slow themselves (see bibliographical note) the following sources have been used in compiling this introduction (Wilts. Cuttings and Wilts. Portraits at W. A. S. Library, Devizes):

1. Books and periodical articles:

"Edward Slow" [obituary and list of writings], in *Wiltshire Archaeological and Natural History Magazine*, vol. 43, 1927, pp. 110–112.

OLIVIER, Edith *Without knowing Mr. Walkley*, 1938, pp. 161–164.

ROGERS, Norman *Wessex dialect*, 1979.

"The seventeenth general meeting . . . held at Wilton", in *Wiltshire Archaeological and Natural History Magazine*, vol. 13, 1872, pp. 1–32.

WILLIAMS, Alfred, "Edward Slow: the Wiltshire dialect poet", in *British Workman*, March 1913.
(Wilts. Portraits, 4.66)

Various Wiltshire and Salisbury trade directories.

2. Newspaper articles:

Salisbury & Winchester Journal, 3.12.1898 (Wilts. Cuttings, 4.487)

Morning Leader, 27.1.1911 (Wilts. Cuttings, 13.194)

[Unidentified 23.10.1913] (Wilts. Cuttings, 16.147)

Salisbury Times, 24.10.1913 (Wilts. Portraits, 4.66)

Salisbury & Winchester Journal, 20.2.1925, p.11.

Salisbury & Winchester Journal, 27.2.1925, p.11.

Salisbury Times, 27.2.1925 (Wilts. Cuttings, 10.134)

Wiltshire Gazette and Herald, 10.11.1966 (Wilts. Cuttings, 23.20)

3. Unpublished sources:

Census enumerators' returns, Wilton, 1841 and 1851.

Wilton parish records (WRO.504).

Selected Poems

THE WILTSHIRE MOONRAKERS.

Down Vizes way zom years, agoo,
When smuggal'n wur nuthen new,
An people wurden nar bit shy,
Of who they did ther sperrits buy.
In a village lived a Publican,
Who kept an Inn, Tha Pelican,
A man he wur, a man a merit
An his neam wur Ickey Perritt.
Ael round about tha country voke
Tha praise of thease yer landlard spoke ;
Var, wen any on 'em wur took bad,
They knaw'd wur sperrits could be had ;
An daly, it wur nice an handy,
At tha Pelican ta get yer brandy.
Twer zwold as chep as tis in Vrance,
Tho a coose, twer done in iggerance.

One winter, Crismis time about,
Thease landlords tubs ad ael run out.
Zays he, this yer's a purty goo,
Var mwore what ever shall I do ;

Thic smugglin Zam's a purty chap,
Ta lave I here wieout a drap;
An wen a promised dree months back,
A hooden vail ta bring me wack.
Bit praps tha Zize voke voun his trail,
An med a pop'd un inta jail,
Howsemdever, I'll zen and zee,
Ta marrer wats became a he.
Zoo next day at nite he off did start,
Two girt chaps wie a donkey cart.
Ta Bristil town thay took ther way,
An got there as twur gettin day;
Tha smugglers house tha zoon voun out,
An tould'n wat they wur com about.
Ael rite, zays he, I've plenty bye,
Bit we mist keep a cuteish eye,
Var tha Zize voke, thay be on tha watch,
An two or dree have lately cotch.
Zoo tell woold Ikey thats tha razin
I cooden zen avore ta pleaz un.
Zoo wen twur dark thase smuggler bwold,
Got dree tubs vrim a zacrit hould;
An unobsarved he purty smart,
Zoon clap'd em in tha donkey cart;
An tha top a cover'd up we hay,
Then sent tha chaps an cart away;
Ael droo tha streets quite zeaf an zoun,
They zoon jog'd out a Bristil town.
An vore tha vull moon ad arose,
To ther neative pleace, wur dràain close

Wen to ther girt astonishment,
They met wie a awkurd accident,
In passin auver Cannins Brudge,
Tha stubborn donkey hooden budge;
Tha chaps thay leather'd well his back,
Bit a diden keer var ther attack;
Bit jibb'd an beller'd, shook his mean
Then kick'd bouth shafts right off za clane.
Up went tha cart, tha tubs vill out,
An in tha road zoon roll'd about;
An vore the chaps cood ardly look,
Ael dree ad roll'd straite in tha brook.
Well! here's a purty goo zays one,
Why Will, wat ever's to be done?
I'd ike ta kill thic donkey quite,
If thee wurst zays Tom, tid zar un rite.
Doost knaa wot tha matter wur?
I thinks a got a vorester;
Var I nevir knaw'd un hack like this,
Unless zummit wur much amiss.
Look at un now he's in a scare,
An gwain as hard as he can tare;
We bouth shafts danglin on tha groun,
A wunt stop till he gets wom I'm bown.
Zoo let un, I dwoant keer a snap,
Var then thay'll gace thease yer mishap;
An zen zumbiddy on tha road,
Ta help ess get wom seaf the load.
Bit zounds, while thus we do delay,
The tubs, begar, ull swim away;

We mist get em out at any price,
Tho tha water be as cwoold as ice.
Dwoant stan geapin zo, var goodness zeak,
Run to thic rick and vind a reak;
I thinks that I can reak em out,
Var ther they be swimmin about.
Two reaks wur got, an then thease two
Did reak and splaish we much ado;
Bit nar a tub thay diden lan,
Thay hooden zeem ta com ta han.
Zays Tom, I'm tired a tha job
An hooden a tuck un var ten bob;
I ad a mine ta let him goo,
An zo I will if thee hoot too.
Get out, girt stup, we mist get in,
Tho we da got wet ta tha skin.
Till never do ta let em be,
Zo tuck thee pants up roun thee knee.
Tha chaps then took tha water bwould,
Tho thay wur shram'd ni we tha cwoold;
And jist as thay did heave one out,
Ael at once a feller loud did shout—
HEL'OH, me lads, wat up to there?
NIGHT POACHERS, ah, if teant I swear.
Let goo, zays Will, I'm blow'd if tent,
Vizes Excizemin on tha scent;
Push off tha tub var goodness zeak,
Get out tha brook, teak hould a reak;
Reak at tha moon a shinin zee,
An dwoant thee spake, I'll tackle he.

Under tha brudge, then out a zight,
Quickly tha tubs wur push'd aelright.

*   *   *   *   *   *

Tha Zizemen now ad rach'd tha pleace,
An Will he draa'd a ruful veace;
We beant no poachers zur zed he,
Bit av ad a mishap as ya zee.
Comin vrim Vize we donkey cart,
On tha brudge tha donk mead zudden start;
An jirk'd, an jib'd, then gied a kick,
An het bwouth shafts off purty quick.
Out went ower things wich as ya zees,
Lays ael about, an yer's a cheese;
He roll'd rite on straite in thease brook,
An Tom's a reakun vor'un look!
Tha Zizeman swallered ael o't in,
And to zee Tom reakun, gun ta grin,
Girt vool, zays he, as true's I'm barn,
Why that's tha moon, thee beest reakun vor'n
An then a busted out agean,
An zed of ael that beat ael clean;
To zee a crazy headed coon,
Reak at the shadder of tha moon.
Will wink'd at Tom, Tom wink'd at Will,
Ta zee how nice he'd took tha pill;
Ah, zur, you med laff as longs ya please,
Bit we be zure it be a Cheese.
Zee, how he shows hisself za plain,
Com Tom, lets reak for he again.

Zoo slap an dash went on tha reakin,
While Zizemin he var vun wur sheakin
An off a went houlden his zide,
Var longer there a cooden bide.
We grinnin his eyes did auvervlow,
Ta zee thay chaps a reakin zo ;
An ta think that now he'd tould em so,
Tha girt vools hooden ther frake vergo.
Zoo up a got apon his hoss,
An as tha brudge a went across,
He zet up another harty grin,
Wen a look'd an zeed em both get in ;
An zed, girt vools, till sar em rite,
If they da ketch ther deaths ta nite.
Bit wen he ad got clane away,
Tha tubs wur got wieout delay ;
And hid away, quite zeaf and zoun,
Var a dark nite, wen tha moon wur down.

* * * * * *

Then at the Pelican thease chaps,
Purty zoon wur tellin ther mishaps ;
Bit ael ther troubles they vergot,
Wen a beer ache om had a pot,
An Ikey coose did pay em well
Thease little stowry not ta tell ;
Zo wen tha Zizemin next did com,
Woold Ikey he a coose wur mum.

An in a glass did jine wie glee,
Wen Zizemin twould tha tale ta he;
Bit he laff'd mwore wen zeaf one nite,
Tha tubs wur brought wom snug an tite:
An many a bumper went around,
To think they'd beat tha Zizemin zound.

*　　*　　*　　*　　*　　*

Bit he tha tale did zoon let out
To ael tha countery roun about;
An to thease day, straingers da teeze,
All Willsheer voke about tha Cheese.
Bit tis thay as can avourd ta grin,
To zee ow nice a wur took in.

*　　*　　*　　*　　*　　*

Zoo, wen out thease County you da goo,
An voke da poke ther vun at you;
An caal ee a girt Willsheer coon,
As went a reakun var tha moon
Jist menshin thease yer leetle stowry,
And then bust out in ael yer glowry,
That, yer cute Excisemen vrum tha town,
Wur took in wie a Willsheer clown.

*　　*　　*　　*　　*　　*

Zoo dwoant ee mine be'n call'd a Mooney,
Twur he, ya zee, as wur tha Spooney.

THA GIRT HARCHEOLOGY.

A main girt fuss ther wur las week,
  In thase yer leetle town, min
Var here did meet a lot a voke,
  Of girt hankshint renown, min.

Bit wat 'twar var, I hardly knows,
  An dall'd, if I can zee ;
This much I knows, they caals therselves,
  Tha girt Harcheology.

Vust day thay in Town Hall did meet,
  As thick as any vlees ;
A viewin on all zart a things,
  Of woold anticketies.

An ther ower Passin rade aloud,
  While zome did nod an snore ;
A peaper, bout ower girt vine Church,
  Which main o'm knaw'd avore.

An ater that, thay went ta dine,
  Down at tha Pembrook Yarms ;
Which wur tha ony thing ta I,
  Tha zeemed ta av zum charms.

Ther thay did stuff an vill away,
  Unger an thirst ta quench ;
Bit wat tha ad, I cudden tell,
  Vor 'twur put down in Vrench.

Then thay did spachefy an zay,
  Wat thay wur gwain to do ;
An zom wur zartin zure that thay,
  Shid vine out zummit new.

Nex day in busses, brakes, an vans,
  Thay went off vor a spree ;
An purty well thay manag'd it,
  Thase girt Harcheology.

Vor everywhere wur thay did goo,
  Nice veasts wur ael spread out ;
Amang tha woold anticketies,
  Which thay wur come about.

We Wardour, they zeem'd nayshun plaz'd,
  As thay wak'd in an out ;
Tha vine woold ruins stannin there,
  Wat Cromwell knock'd about.

Nex day thay off agean did goo,
  To Zalsbry an aroun ;
Ta zee tha girt vine hankshint things,
  That ael about is voun.

An ael did look za jolly well,
An plaz'd as thay could be ;
Var skierce bit veasten ael tha time,
Be thase Harcheology.

Bit as I zed avore, I dwoant,
An even now caant zee ;
Wat good thay dooes ta we poor voke,
Thase girt Harcheology.

Ta zee woold ruins an woold things,
Na doubt ta thay zeems gran ;
Bit dang if I dwont think that thay,
Cud, het on a better plan.

Za-poussin thay wur ael ta meet,
Ta renevate tha ruin ;
Of poor vokes houssen that thay zees,
Wat good ud thay be do-un.

Bit spoose var drownin' out thease hint,
I mist apologie ;
Bit I da hope thay'll ze ta it,
Thase girt Harcheology.

*   *   *   *   *

Of this I spoose you've ad anuff,
Zoo I'll draa it to a close ;
If mwore about em you do want,
Rade Bob Burn's Captin Grose !

ZONG.

THA COT ON ZALSBRY PLAAIN.

Me fiather is a shepherd bwold,
  An lives on Zalsbry Plaain ;
Vrim marn till nite he tends his sheep,
  In wind, an starm, and rain ;
Tho loanely be his humble lot,
  He never do complain,
Var sweet contentment vills tha cot
  Away on Zalsbry Plaain!

CHORUS :—

O tha leetle thatch roof cot,
  Wur happiness da reign ;
Of ael plazin in tha wordle gie I
  Tha cot on Zalsbry Plaain !

Me mother, dear, God bless her heart,
Wat she've a done vor I
Da meak me heart rise in me brist,
An tears rin in me eye;
Var wen I left me happy wom
Wat woe an bitter pain
Did vill her up tha day I left
Tha cot on Zalsbry Plaain!

O tha leetle thatch roof cot, &c.

A brawny zailor bwold I'm now,
I've brav'd tha starmy sea,
In a Man-a-war, ta zarve me Queen,
Likewise me countery;
An offen in tha zilent nite,
Apon tha voamin main,
Wat drames av com into me yead
Of tha cot on Zalsbry Plaain!

O tha leetle thatch roof cot, &c.

I've zailed aelroun tha wordle twice,
I've bin in every clime,
I've had zim crosses, an I've had
Zim pleasures in me time;
Bit this I zays amang it ael,
Tha pleasures and tha pain,
Tha bright gem that wur uppermwoast
Wur tha cot on Zalsbry Plaain!

O tha leetle thatch roof cot, &c.

Bit now me time is draaen on,
  An in a year or two
I'll be discharged, an then I'll get
  A pinchin as me due;
To shipmeats then I'll bid varewell,
  Varewell to ocean's main;
Here's hoff ta get another berth
  In tha cot on Zalsbry Plaain.

    O tha leetle thatch roof cot, &c.

An ah! wat joy till be var I
  Ta greet me parients kine;
Ta rove about in they woold haunts
  I now can caal ta mine;
Ta veel I'm vree of ael tha wordle,
  Once mwore a Wiltshire swain;
Ta live, an die, an raste me bounes,
  Near tha cot on Zalsbry Plaain!

    O tha leetle thatch roof cot,
      Wur happiness da reign;
    Of ael plazin in tha wordle gie I
      Thic cot on Zalsbry Plaain!

THA GIRT VAT PIG.

Ower fiather's gwain ta kill tha pig,
When he comes wom ta-night;
An lore tha thoughts on it da vill
I up we mad delight.

Tho we shill miss poor Toby much,
A grunten in his stye;
Bit mother zays tha beakin's gone,
An we caant avord ta buy.

Zides, Toby now is vat, an vit,
He's purty nigh ten scoure;
Two baigs a barleymeal he've had,
A mussen av no mwore.

Zoo ta Toby we mist zay varewell,
Of grub he've had his wack;
Na mwore we'll car un extry bits,
Na mwore we'll scratch his back.

Ah 'tis a appy time a twoam
Wen we da kill a pig,
Var zich nice veasten I da av,
Wich meaks I grow za big.

Var I avs ael his pettitoes,
An girt black puddens vine,
Mother da meak, an vagots too,
An chidlins much's I mine.

Mwoast every day, var two ar dree weeks
Wie avs zich nice pig's vry;
Wich meaks I run about and zing—
" What a happy bwoy be I."

On Zundys, too, mother da roast
A nice girt bit a griskin,
Which som da like mworn butcher's mate,
Begar, an zo da I min.

An then we puts his vine vat zides
Into a girt big zilt;
An well wie zalt we rubs em droo,
Till inta brine da milt.

An there we lets em bide a bit,
Till thay be well zoak'd droo;
Then out we teaks em, an da hang
Em up tha chimley vlue.

Up thayre they bides a smoken nice,
Till thame as browns a berry;
An lore ta zee em hangin there
Meaks fiather zart a merry.

An when thame dry a piece we cuts,
Var bwilen, ar var raishers;
An fiather cuts out bouth tha hams,
A pair a regler slaishers.

An ther ache zide tha vire-pleace,
  Thay bouth da hang za brown,
Zo's ta be ready var ta cook,
  When Jack an Poll comes down.

Var tho thay livs in Lunnen town,
  An can av butcher's mate;
Heet they bouth vows as fiather's ham
  Ta thay's a bigger trate.

Zoo every Club ar Crismis time,
  A ham gooes inta pot;
Var ower vamly reckens ten,
  A main girt ungry lot.

I warn thic bwone is polished off
  Avore thay gooes away;
Which fiather's aelwys plazed to zee,
  Da meak his woold heart gay.

An mother she is aelwys plazed
  Ta zee ower appetite;
"Tis purty zartin zure," she zaays,
  "Yer bellies be ael right."

Sparkle wie jay me eyes thay do,
  Ta zee a ham on teable;
Var aelwys I da av ta ate
  As much as I be yeable.

Var mother she da zarve it out,
  Cos she can carve za quick;
An well she knaas I likes it long,
  An nar bit nice how thick.

Let gennelvoke cry up their geam,
  Their vensin, veal, ar lam;
Bit var a nunch jist let I av
  A nice girt chunk a ham.

An this I zaays ta wirken voke,
  If a meal ya wants a good un,
Cook a ham, an lots a gierden stuff,
  An a nice girt figgy pooden.

An if that ar dwoant vill ee up,
  An try a bit yer buttons,
I'm zarten zure that nuthen wunt,
  Ar else ya be girt gluttons.

Ta leabouren voke tis a girt thing
  Ta av a pig in stye;
Var he'll turn many a shillin in,
  Wen he is vat, bim bye.

An many a teasty bit he'll av,
  Ta putt apon his plate;
Var well we knaa he caant avourd
  Ta buy no butcher's mate.

I wish that every leabouren man
  Had a gierden nice an big,
An a leetle stye, kept nice and clane,
  An many a girt vat pig.

POLL'S WEDDIN.

'Twur in tha zunny month a May,
  Wen birds da zweetly zing,
That Jackey Bell, of yonder dell,
  Ta Church ower Poll did bring.
An nevir in me life av I
  Enjayed mezelf za well
As wen ower Poll got married to
  Young strappin Jackey Bell.

We ael got up at vower o'clock,
  An bustled zo about,
Ta get things ready vor tha veast,
  A proper gran turn out.
Lore ow we trim'd tha woold house up,
  We evergreens an vlowers,
Girt lims we stuck agean tha door,
  Ta form zim sheady bowers.

At breakfist time, lore, how we chaff'd
Poor Poll about her man,
Bit then she know'd twur ony jokes,
Vor she coud understan.
An fiather jok'd and zed "zappose
Young Jackey shuden come,
Why Poll, what ever hood ee do?
What ever hood be done?"

An Poll laughed out an zed, "zappose
Ta Church I hooden goo,
Wad shud ee think a that, now zay,
Whatever hood ee do?
But lack a day, no vear a that,
I shall be his ta day,
Vor he da like I much ta well
Ta think ta bide away."

An while we wur a chaffin so
A rap com to tha door,
An Poll rush'd up ta open un,
Twur Jackey she wur sure.
An twur, begar, an wat a zite,
He claps hur roun tha wease,
An gied hur kisses, sich a lot,
Ael bout her rozy feace.

Lore, ow we laff'd an cried, vor joy,
Ta zee thick two together;
"God bless em bouth," zed Granny out,
"Ther love may nothin zever."

An poor young Jan tha tears rin'd out
  His eyes vor very joy,
Then poor woold Granfer hollerd out
  "God bless ee, maid an bwoy."

Zo now tha time wur gettin on,
  Tha maids thay went up stair,
Ta put ther bran new dresses on,
  An trim an plat their hair.
An Jackey he went long a I,
  Ta dress hisself za gran,
Var I wur gwain, doont ee zee, to act
  As Jackey Bell's baste man.

Wen ael wur ready, out we went,
  Zix couples in tha train,
An twur a nayshin purty zite,
  As I shant zee again;
Tha maids they wur done up in gowns,
  That shined jist like zilk,
Tha chaps in black trowjers an cwoats,
  An weasecuts white as milk.

Ael down tha village street we went,
  Lar ow tha voke did stear,
A underd voices did cry out
  "God bless ee, Polly dear;"
Tha men voke, too, they ad their zay
  As geanst tha church they stuck,
As we went droo thay ael did zay
  "Mine keep yer sperrits up."

Tha Passin then begun ta rade
  Tha zarvice var tha weddin,
An fiather gied poor Poll away,
  While mother tears wur sheddin.
Wen Passin ax'd young Jan, if he
  Hood av Poll var a wife,
In a loud voice, a zed a hood,
  An stick ta she droo life.

Then joyfully we lav'd tha Church,
  As appy as anything,
An ael at once tha bells begun
  Za merrily ta ring;
An we march'd back like voke in steat,
  Amang tha vok's hooray;
Zuch welcomes then thay gied thick two,
  Their blessed wedding day.

Then down we zat ta dinner gran,
  Roun fiather's oaken teable,
An everything wur thur ta ate,
  As much as you wur yeable.
A junk a beef, a woppin ham,
  A nice girt laig a mutten,
Puddens an tearts, ther wur anuff
  Ta zatisfy a glutton.

An ater that wur cleard away,
  Ael zarts a fruit we ad,
Vigs, Apples, Nuts, an Oranges,
  An yale, ta meak ess glad.

An there we bid var dree long hours,
An ael za jolly appy,
Tha young uns thay did dance and zing,
Tha woold uns blow'd their baccy.

Then mother did perpose a plan,
An this wat she did zay—
"Now ael o'ee teak a walk down street,
While I da clare away."
An straite our things we bustled on,
An march'd ael down tha street,
An ael our vrens we did invite,
At zix a'clock ta meet.

Zo at zix a'clock they ael did meet
In uncle's girt lang barn,
Vor there we wur ta ave a ball,
An keep un up till marn.
An ower brass band, they did get up
In a waggon tother end,
An they did play zo nice an loud,
Zich musick out did zend.

A cask a cider an a beer
We'd roll'd into tha barn,
Which uncle ad zend down ta we,
A present vrom the varm.
Zo everything wur ready now
An vrens they ael wur com,
"Lead off tha dance" zed fiather then,
An bang then went tha drum!

An in two rows ael down the barn,
  Tha men an maidens stood,
To've zeed ess there, I'm zure it hood
  Av done yer heart much good.
Vor Jan an Poll stood on tha top,
  An wen tha ban did zoun,
They did lead off in purty style,
  Thic woold dance, vower ans roun.

Zo we did dance, an joke an zing,
  Vor hours thick weddin nite,
An raaly there ta zee ess ael,
  It wur a fectin zite.
Vor ael wur cheer an harminy,
  Amang ess, young an woold,
Twur jist like one big vamily,
  Zich vrenship we did hold.

An I da hope wen I da wed,
  Ta keep me weddin zo,
Vor I da think, then ael good voke
  Their kindness ought ta show ;
Vor 'tis a time, a time a cheer.
  We girt voke an we small,
An wen I weds jist let I have
  A weddin like our Poll.

GIPSYUN AT STOUNEHENGE.

One day ower Dick, an I, an Tom,
  Wic Cousin Jean and Meary Ann,
An two ar dree mwore vrim up tha hill
  Did het upon a goodish plan.

Vor we agreed we'd goo an zee
  Tha girt big stounes out at Stounehenge,
An av a proper jolly spree,
  An jay owerzelves wie ael ower vrens.

Zo ache o's wur to 'vite a vren,
  To meak a purty leetle pearty,
An ael agreed ta pay za much,
  Ta meak tha day zo nice and harty.

Zo wen ael o't wur zettled down,
  Away we zent ower Meary Ann,
Ta ax woold Uncle if he'd lend
  His hosses an his girt spring van.

An Uncle wur za martil plazed,
  He zed he'd drave ess wur we mind,
An hooden charge ess not a vig,
  Var his woold heart be true an kind.

Zo wen tha day wur drawin ni,
  There wur zich fussen mang the maids,
A meaken zich girt pies an cakes,
  Ta want we wur nar bit avraid.

A girt big piece of beef they'd cook'd,
  An zich a woppin ham had bought,
They wur abliged ta cut un droo,
  Ta get un in tha biggest pot.

An Tom, tha hostler, vrom tha "Boot,"
  Ad brought a cask of frothen beer,
An one a leetle less than he,
  Sim stingo that ud meak ee queer.

Zo auver nite we put it ael
  In readiness ta com ta han,
Vor Uncle zed he shood be here
  At nine o'clock wie hoss an van.

Nar bit a sleep we ad thic nite,
  A thinkin bout tha comin day,
An vore tha zun we bundled up,
  Vor longer there we cooden lay.

Zo bye an bye we zoon did spy
  Woold Uncle comin on tha rouad,
An by tha time tha clock struck ten,
  We ad got up mwoast ael ower louad.

An we ad deck'd up Uncle's van,
  Wie vlowers and ribbons ael about,
Then off we went wie hearts so lite,
  An mang tha people's cheers an shout.

An we did ride alang za vine,
  Apon tha rouad towards the Stounes,
An ony stopp'd apon tha hills
  To raste a bit tha hosses bounes.

An bye an bye, tha Stounes appeared,
  Jist like tha trunks a holler trees,
Vor ta look at they a girt way off,
  Tis a nation curious zite ta zee.

An wen we draa'd a leetle nier,
  Like giants they did zeem to stan,
Var every sheap an varm they looks,
  A stanin on thick piece a lan.

Zoo atter joggetten about
  Auver tha roads an auver mounds,
By tha Stounes we hetched tha hosses out
  An let em run about tha downs.

Come now, zed Uncle, lets a zee
  Wat ya av brought vor we to ate,
Var I da veel mwoast mortal leer,
  An zo get out tha brade an mate.

Zo Fan did spread a girt big cloth
  Apon tha grass, an we zat down,
An mead shart wirk of beef an ham,
  Vor appetites we ael ad voun.

An we did ate and drink za long,
  Till nothing skierce wur left bit bounes,
Then up we got ta look about,
  An zee tha girt big hankshint Stounes.

An Fan an I, wie nub a chaak,
  Did meak a mark za big an white,
Ta zee if we cud count em ael—
  Dang if cud count em twice alike.

Then Uncle zed as how thase Stounes
  Wur stuck up yer in midnight revel,
Bit some da zay they must av bin
  Stuck up here by woold Nick, tha D—l.

An zom da think it wur tha sae
  Wur our leetle land da bide,
An that thase Stounes wur drifted up
  Ta where they be we ocean's tide.

An zom da zay they wur put up
  Like martar, ael za slack and soft,
An ardened wie tha han a time,
  An winds, an starms, an girt hard vrost.

But I da think as Uncle zed—
  They mist av com wie thick woold fellar,
Vor zomehow, I da zeem ta think
  I yeard un, under one o'm bellar.

But, howsemdever, ther they stans,
  A nayshin hard and stubborn group,
An even they girt Archeyoligist,
  I'm dang if they can meak em out.

Zo atter we ad gap'd about,
  An zeed ael that ther wur ta zee,
Ache one did teak his peertener
  Ta av a leetle bit a spree.

Then cousin Tom begun a teun
  On a viddle stuck below his chin,
An we begun ta jump about—
  Lore, how we mead woold Uncle grin.

Tid mead ee laff, ad you bin there,
  Ta zee tha keapers we did cut;
'Twur nuff ta meak a passin laff
  Ta zee ess in thic vine kick up.

An when wie wur mwoast tired out,
  We zat down in tha stounen ring,
An Fan an I begun a teun,
  An ael het in, to help and zing.

An then Jem Smith, a artful chap,
  Did zing about a chap in Lunnen,
Who did get rob'd of ael a had
  Up there, we voke za martil cunnin.

An 'twur a proper vunny zong,
  It nearly mead wie split ower zides,
Ta hear tha things he did goo droo,
  Vor, girt fool, he belived ther lies.

Zo ache a we did zing a zong,
An merrily did pass tha time,
An uncle he did finish up
Be zingin "Days a Woold Lang Syne."

At dark we put tha hosses in,
An jogged along athirt tha plaain;
'Twur twelve a'clock avore we ael
Ad got back to our woms again.

An jolly plazed wur every one,
I do assure ee, my good vrens,
An I do hope next hallerday
We'll goo agean ta woold Stounehenge.

SMILIN JACK:

A TRUE STOWRY OF A MIDNIGHT ADVENTER.

Thease stowry I be gwain to tell
Is zartin true, I mines un well,
It happened wen I wur a bwoy,
In pinnyfores an carderoy;
Var broad cloth wurden wore much then
Be leetle bwoys, nar neet be men.
Well! in thease town ther lived a chap
Who kept a donkey an a trap,
Which he used in his hawkin trade,
An, be wich he lots a money made;
Tha voke ael caal'd un Smilin Jack,
Becaus a ad a happy knaek
Wen buyin ar zillen anything
Ta laff an whissle, joke, ar zing,
Voke zed it wur his artvul craff
Ta teak em in, then meak em laff,
Cos a vunny tale he'd always spin
Wen their good graces he hood win;
Howzemdever, wur twur zo ar not
A proper good trade he'd a got,

Var twenty miles, he wur vound
In every village, ael a round,
At markits too, an country vairs,
There he wur zeed, hawkin his wares.
Anything amwoast he'd buy and zill,
Zo's it did bring grist to his mill,
An tho wie voke a bargin'd hard,
They looked on un wie zom regard
Aelthough we wit, an joke, za vunny
A wiggled them out a ther money.
Now it come ta pass one Whitzuntide
Jack, he wur ax'd var to perzide
At a club veast, near Huminten,
Cos auver there liv'd mwoast his kin.
Good custumers did there rezide,
And twur his neative wom bezide,
Zoo a zent ta zay a hood be thayre
In weather vowl, ar weather fayre.

Tha day arrived, an Smilin Jack
Mounted upon his donkey's back,
Ael rig'd in one of his best suits,
Wie spurs a stickin vrum his boots,
Went gallopin ael droo tha town,
Like zom girt hero of renown,
And many wur tha shouts and cheers,
As he rode off, did greet his ears;
Var everybiddy it wur plain
Wanted ta knaa wur he wur gwain.
Bit a thay, ower hero took no heed
Bit galloped on his way we speed.

At tha girt hill caal'd Bishopstone,
He there dismounted vrom his throne,
An led his Neddy up tha steep,
Vor'd got a heart, as cood veel deep,
Tho' in zom things a wur abused,
His vaithvul donk, he neer ill-used.
Zom zed Ned ad a aiseyer life
An knaa'd mwore kindness than Jack's wife.

Tha top zoon gained, donkey an he
Did rache tha village speedily;
An as thay jog'd ael down tha street,
Tha village voke turn'd out ta greet
An welcom Jack we cheervul smile,
Var adden bin ther zich a while.
Tha bells thay rung, tha ban did play,
Acos it wur tha club veast day.
An clubmen ael drest in ther best
Hasten'd ta sheak hands we ther guest.
Then down along ta "Vox an Goose"
He hies, ta zet his donkey loose,
An ta refresh his parched inzide
Atter thic lang an dusty ride.

Then atter church, tha veast is spread,
An ower hero at tha teables yead
Caals down a blessin on tha vood,
Ta do ther souls an bodies good.
Justice wur done, I need'n state
Ta every man's well laden plate,
Var ael who've dined at a country club
Knaas purty well, how vlees tha grub,

Var thease poor men not every day
Vrim a prime jint can cut away.
As var tha drink, I cooden zay
How many quarts wer stowed away
Be ache, an every clubman there,
Who drunk till's eyes begun to stare.

Time vlew along, still at tha head,
Ower hero, Jack, maintains tha lead.
He cracks his jokes, swigs ael an grog,
An issues vorth a droll prologue.
Glass atter glass, da disappear,
Tha teables groan we grog an beer.
Boozin an smokin on thay go
We yeads a bobbin to an vro,
An like a zombre vuneral pall
Tha thick smoke hangs aroun tha wall;
Zweethearts, an wives, an children young,
Like sheep at vair be ael among,
Nigh chokin we tha fumes a baccy,
Yet mang tha din zeeminly happy.
A snatch of a zong, a chorus ar two
Tha hours away like lightnin vlew.
Jack, like a king, zits ael tha while
An skierce thinks on, tha vive lang mile,
Nar thic drary ride across tha plain
Avore he can rache wom again.
We drink an smoke, he neer is blind,
A total blank da zeem his mind,
He've lost ael power ta stan upright,
Prostrate, an auvercom he's quite.

Tis nearly twelve, tha Host coms in
An baals out mang tha naisy din,
"Tha time is up, ya ael must go
Ar I'll lose me license as ya know."
Another zong, they ael did shout,
We'll av, avore we do turn out.
One vrim tha cheerman, thay did baal,
An Jack tried to ablige ther caal.
But he wur done, gone wur his pow'r,
An up a got, nettled an zower.
An blarin out this yer wunt do,
I mist me journey now pursue.
Here Ossler Tom, bring roun me ass,
An Lanlard here, jist one mwore glass.
He drained another, vill ta ground,
Var he wur drunk, an that vull zound,
His donk jist then appeared in zite,
He mounts an wish em ael "goodnight,"
Then gallop'd vast ael down tha street
Like a scalded pig a did retreat.
Tha toll geat swung back in a trice,
Tha toll man baal'd out var tha price,
But Jack vur up tha road wur gone,
Tha geat man cooden vollie on,
Bit swore that Jack another day
Double tha toll hood av ta pay.
Tha vaithvul donkey up tha hill
Did trot away we right good will.
Poor brute, he wur a honest ass,
An well know'd his rider had a glass.

Ta Jack tha road appear'd ta waak,
He sway'd like to a tender staak ;
He'd lost the power his donk ta guide
An tha usual track he missed wide.
Aware of thease unusual route
Ned o'er tha down an vields did scout,
Way down ta water medders green,
Where Jack got conscious of tha scene,
Zoo gien he a sharp pull round
He drow'd his rider to tha ground
An be tha zide of a muddy ditch,
Ower muddled hero he did pitch ;
He scrabbled up, wen zummat new,
A ghost-like varm appeared in view,
It vlitted here, it vlitted there,
Then zeem'd ta vanish in tha air,
Quite dazed, a now began ta think
That he mist be tha wuss var drink.

A thunder storm, now gathered thick
An in tha gloom appear'd woold Nick
Wie harns, an hoofs, an hissin tail,
Tha zite o't mead un quake an quail.
Eyes big as saacers, rid as vire,
Wie awe their victim, did inspire,
His claas held ard a two grain'd prong
An a beckon'd Jack ta come along.
Ower hero's hair stood bolt an end
As he look'd at thick foul fiend,
Wie vrite a vairly stood agast
An tried ta run, bit's laigs stuck vast

Trimblin a stood like a broken reed
Var zich a zite he'd never zeed.
His poor woold ass he loud did bray,
While Jack vill on his knees ta pray,
An promisin what 'ee hood do
In futer, if he'd let un goo.
As var tha drink, dear zur, I mean
Never ta touch tha stuff agean,
Var tis me ony bane in life,
An gets me inta endless strife
Zides wurryin, me poor dear wife.

Tha thunder now begun ta roar,
Lightnin tha clouds azunder tore,
An big rain drops begun ta vall
Vrim murky clouds, as black's a pall.
Wis ever man in zich a plight
As ower hero, on thick dreadvul night.
Prayin ta heavin fervently
Vrum thease enemy to zet un vree.
Vull haaf a nower there a knelt,
Till down amain tha starm did pelt,
An as it wash'd his parched brow,
New life zeem'd to poor Jack endow.
Then up a got an peer'd around,
Ole Nick had vanish'd under ground.
Loudly Jack baal'd out vur his ass
Who unconsarned ved on tha grass.
At last Ned ansers to his beck,
Jack cuddles un aroun tha neck.

Then mounts agean, hopen that he
Vrim vurther mishap shood be vree.
Droo mead a rach'd tha turnpike track,
Thank God I'm seaf zaays Smilin Jack.
Once mwore, zays he, I be aelright,
As tha well know'd Park appear'd in zite.
Then joggin ael down by tha wall
Holden Ned's ears zo's not ta vall.
Grazed be tha trees, an bramble scratches,
A neer had rach'd tha vourteen hatches
When ha, another trouble zore
Did meet un, wuss than he avore.
His donk on nearen tha long brudge
Zuddently to tha stream did trudge,
An vore his tention, Jack cood drame,
He'd shook un off, right in the strame ;
Then away did scamper quick as thought
As tho ee hooden agean be caught,
Nar did er slack his pace avore
A stood in front his owner's door.

Vloundern an splashen in tha wave,
Jack struggled hard dear life ta save,
He rach'd tha edge, vill on tha baink
Cussin his donkey's purty praink.
Coold an wet droo to tha skin,
An veelin vaint an bad within,
He tried to waak but vill to ground
An pray'd that zoon a med be vound.

*　　*　　*　　*　　*　　*

His wife stopped up var un thick night,
Bit went ta bade dreamt ael was right,
Thinkin he'd drain'd an extry cup
An till nex day hooden turn up.
Bit at marn, wen she undid tha door
Tha loanly donkey stood avore,
Wieout measter, bridle, or bit,
Wurden she jist in a purty clit,
"Wurs thy measter, woold vool," she zed,
"Hast thee a left un, live ar dead?"
Bit tha donkey shook his yead, an bray'd,
Much as to say a idden slay'd.
Betty, zoon rais'd a hue an cry,
An naybours purty quick did hie.
O dear! O dear! alack! alack!
What is become a' Smilin Jack?
Tha hunted here, tha hunted there,
To Huminten zom did repair.
Vrens an relayshins vill'd tha cot,
Ael o'm lamontin poor Jack's lot,
Var zure ta hear he'd broke his neck
Mwoast every one o'm did expec.
Poor Betty, she did heave a zigh,
An purty zoon did pipe her eye.
"An is er now var ever gone,
An must I widder's weeds put on?
Poor Jack, wat ever shill I do,
Thee wurst a usbin kind, an true."
An as her loss she did deplore
She yeard zim shoutin at tha door,

Var up did drive woold Tommy Bawter
Who'd vound our Jack down be tha water,
Close ta tha brudge, at vourteen hatches,
Ael cover'd o'er we blood an scratches.
He'd brought un wom, snug in his trap,
An baalin out cried, "rouse up Jack."
Ower hero woke, then rushed in doors
Amid tha people's laffin roars,
He rolled ta bed an slep vull zound,
An dram'd a wur in water drown'd.

It done un good, var zunce thick day
Vrim strong drink, he have kept away,
Aelthough a offen gets a rub,
Bout wen a din'd at Huminten club,
An thick are awful night za drear
Wen woold Nick to un, did appear.

THA WOOLD GROVELY VOX.

Ther's a crafty woold vox, up in Grovely hood,
An as gray as a vox well can be,
An he's roamin about, vrim marnen till night,
An I'm dang if nooan o'm can ketch he.

CHORUS.

Var lightly a trips it, and merrily bounds,
An keers not var huntsmin, neet narn a ther hounds.

He knaas every thicket, he knaas every nook,
He da knaa every hole in the ground;
The cunnen woold baiger, knaas jist wur to hide
When the huntsmin his harn da jist zound.

CHORUS.

Var lightly a trips it, an merrily bounds,
An keers not var huntsmin, neet narn a ther hounds.

Hache varmstead he da knaa, bouth zides a tha hood,
An nightly down there he da prowl,
An many a varmer, vust thing in tha marn,
Da miss a vat duck or a vowl.

CHORUS.

An away we his booty, right merry he bounds,
An keers not var varmers, nar huntsmin, nar hounds.

Two vine lots a hounds, var ten years an mwore
Av bin on tha woold baiger's track,
To a nice leetle dance he've a led em oftimes,
An defied the whole vield an ther pack.

CHORUS.

Var lightly a trips it, an merrily bounds,
An keers not var huntsmin, neet narn a ther hounds.

Bwold Vreemin, an Stovin, oft puzzled their brains.
  Var ta bring thease geam rascal ta bay,
An tho' many times thay av press'd un zore,
  A did manidge ta bid em good-day.

CHORUS.

Var lightly a trips it an merrily bounds,
An keers not var huntsmin, neet narn a ther hounds.

Ther's blunt keeper Hine, an his butty Bill Noyce,
  As droo hood every day thay da jog.
Da oft com across'n, bit tha woold baiger knaas
  They wont touch un wie gun nar wie dog.

CHORUS.

An vrom em he trips it, an merry he bounds,
An dwoant keer var keepers, nar huntsmin nar hounds.

An tho he da rob em of many a bird,
  Vat phesant is a nice dainty snack,
He da knaa be tha laa, he's zacred to ael,
  Zeave tha measter, tha huntsmin, an's pack.

CHORUS.

An vrom em he trips it, an merry he bounds,
An dwoant keer var keepers, nar huntsmin, nar hounds.

Lard Radner declares he'll av un zom day,
  We a vair an a square spourtsmin kill,
An tho he'ev kotch one, heet thease crafty woold vox,
  Up in Grovely's a wanderin still.

CHORUS.

Then hurrah var thease vox, who merrily bounds,
An dwoant keer var huntsmin, neet narn a ther hounds.

THA GIRT BIG FIGGETTY POODEN.

Ah, wen I wur a girt hard bwoy,
We appetite nar mossel coy,
Tha baste thing out ta gie I joy,
  Wur a girt big figgetty pooden.

Tha very neam ow'un zeem'd anuff
An ta smill un, ow did meak I puff,
An lor, ow I did vill an stuff,
  When mother mead a pooden.

Hache birthday she wur sure ta meak,
A girt plum pooden, an a keak,
An ax a vew vrens to parteak,
  Of her nice figgetty pooden.

Tho mother adden much ta spend
She mead un good ya may depend,
An purty quick ther wur a end,
  A thick ar birthday pooden.

Na vear a any on't getten stale,
If I wur handy an wur hale,
Me appetite hood never vail,
  As long as ther wur pooden.

Not that I wur a girt big glutton
Like thic chap, as ate a laig a mutton,
Tho me waiscut oft I did unbutton
  When twur a extry girt un.

When I wur in tha village choir,
An a veast wur gied ess be tha Squire,
Tha us'd ta com in ael a vire,
  An as black mwoast as me hat.

An twur rare vun to zee em smoke,
Var in wine an brandy they did zoak,
An pon me zong it wur no joke,
  Aten much a that ar pooden.

Var mezelf I'd zooner av em plain,
Zo's you can cut an com again,
Wieout tha dread a gien ee pain,
  Like tha there brandy poodens.

Wen in ta Zalsbry oft I went,
Var measter on a errant zent,
I warn, mwoast ael me brass wur spent,
  In buyin zim figgetty pooden.

I used ta knaa a leetle shop,
In Brown Street, wur I off did pop,
An well vill up me ungry crop,
  We nice sweet figgetty pooden.

Tha used ta beak em in a tin,
An tha ooman she did offen grin,
Ta zee ow zoon I did ate in
  Her nice hot figgetty pooden.

Times on times we vun she've cried,
An wur ablidgèd ta hould her zide,
Ta zee ow zoon away I'd hide,
  That ar dree penneth a pooden.

It done her good she did declare,
Ta zee I ate me pooden there,
An she aelways gied I mwourn me shear,
  Cos I wur vond a pooden.

Ah, oft I thinks apon tha time,
When Crismis bells merry da chime,
What a girt pooden, nice an prime,
  Mother did meak var we.

A used ta come in steamin hot,
Noarly as big's a waishen pot.
Wie vigs an currands zich a lot,
  In thick ar Crismis pooden.

Lore, ow me young eyes glissen'd at un,
An fiather he did zay, "Odd drat un,"
I do believe while I wur chatten,
  Thick bwoy ud ate thic pooden.

Dree sorrens on't I aelwys had,
An fiather he did look like mad,
Bit mother she wur aelwys glad,
  An zay "Lar let'n av his pooden."

A coose, I diden av much mate,
Nar gierden stuff apon me plate,
An pooden aelwys wur a trate,
Specily thick one at Crismis.

Tho I own, I did av mworn me wack,
Me lips var mwore did offen smack,
An me waistcut offen wur main slack,
Wen tha pooden wur ael gone.

A contented bwoy I aelways wur,
An diden cry an meak a stur,
Wen he wur gone cos there wurnt mwore,
Like a bwoy I knaas who did.

His mother once mead a girt pooden,
Thinkin she'd gie her bwoy a dooin;
Atter aten till na mwore a cooden,
Cry'd, cos a adden vinish'd un.

Wen I grow'd up a biggish bwoy,
Wat thay calls a hobbledehoy,
Tha chaps did try I to annoy
Be caalin out "Figgetty pooden."

Bit there I diden use ta keer,
Var ael ther chaff, an joke, an sneer,
I diden stop it, never vear,
Wen ther wur any pooden.

If ever I da av a wife,
Ta live wie I ael droo thease life,
I'll tell her, if she dwoant want strife,
Ta meak I plenty a poodens.

Begar, I hooden mind betten a crown,
That if a chap is mainly down,
Nuthen ull cure un I'll be bown,
  Like a girt big figgetty pooden.

A zeems ta drave ael keer away,
An meak yer heart veel light an gay,
That you'll zeem merry ael tha day
  Atter aten figgetty pooden.

Zoo teak thease hint ael labourers wives
If you da wish var happy lives,
You'll av em zure, if you contrives
  Ta get lots a figgetty poodens.

If ya caant avoord much butcher's mate,
Ta putt apon yer husbin's plate,
Putt avore un then, what he can ate,
  A nice girt figgetty pooden.

His health an straingth it will zustain,
An vlesh he's zartin zure to gain,
An a unger never he'll complain,
  If ya gets un lots a pooden.

Meself, ael things I hood gie up,
Even do wieout me pipe an cup,
Var I cud dinner, tay, an zup.
  On a nice girt figgetty pooden.

OWER GIRT ZEPTEMBER VAIR.

Of ael naizes an zenes in tha country that are,
Ther's nuthen ta beat ower girt Zeptember vair;
Var hussle, an bussle, an tussle, we man an wie be-ast,
It can vie wie any in tha country at least.
Now if ya da dout it, com an zee var yer-zelf,
An be here day avore, Zeptember tha twelth;
When about dinner time ya zure will begin,
Ta hear indycashions of tha vorth comin din.
Then on tha vair marn of tha clock about two,
Outzid a yer dwoor ye'll hear much ado;
That is, if you'm sleepen in tha nayberhood too,
An beant zunk too deep in a girt snorin stew.
You'll turn, an you'll twis, an mutter what's this?
An agean try to zink in slumberin bliss;
Then praps var a nower, you med get a snooze,
Ael depens, ta wither much naise you've been used.

But wither or not, agean about vour, you'll zadly deplore,
That vor tha naize at yer door,
Tha bussle an roar, ya raaly caant snore,
An praps in a bore you'll turn oer an oer,
Ta get a wink more.
But you'll vind tis useless, an that you'll convess, as ya jump up an dress in half drowsiness.

Wen dress'd, about vive,
In tha street you arrive;
Which is ael alive,
Like bees in a hive;
An mabby you'll contrive
At tha vair to arrive;
If hardly ya strive,
Mang tha bussle ta dive;
An goo in an out, like a rickety wheel,
Ar like country chaps a dancen a reel.
But wen wonce at the vair,
Dang if you wunt declare.
You wurd'nt aware,
Twur zich an affair.
An mainly you'll stare,
To zee voke here an there,
Run like mad everywhere,
As tho in a scare,
Be the steat of their hair,
An ther eyes wen they stare;
Tis a terryable glare,
Nuthun can we it compare.

Ta hear varmers a shoutin, an scoutin, an poutin,
Especially fat ones, that have got tha gout in;
An shepperds a tearin, an swearin, an blarin,
An dogs a prowlin, an howlin, an growlin;
At ther poor leetle vlock, ta get em in dock, avore zix o'clock,
Ar vore there's a block.
Jist hark at their slang,
In ther neative twaing;
Well, I'm dang, if there the beant, ael amang.

Poor gentle sheep, var you I veels deep, as tho I cood weep,
Ta zee ee zo huddled ael up in a heap,
That too wie out keep;
An there to remain var howrs in yer pain,
I knaa you hood fain be away on tha plain,
We nuthen to restrain on tha grassy domain;
Wie no hurry, or skurry, or strainge curs ta wurry.

* * * * * *

Wat a rum zite is thease vair at its hite;
Wat things ta ex-zite'ee, wat zouns ta a-vrite'ee;
Wat feacin ya zee, zom beamin wie glee,
An on others ther be lines a adversety;
An ael zems bent on, business intent on.
Tha gennelmin varmer here ya da meet,
In tha latest fayshun, nate an complate;
An tha woold fayshun yoman,
Who'd av ya ta know, man,
That he beant a show man;

Be his plain zimple dress,
Yer mine he'll himpress
That he do possess
Much straite foridness.
Zee thay yander together,
In ther laggins a leather
Hearts lite as a veather,
Discussen tha weather;
Tha sheep, an ther keep;
Tha carn, in tha barn;
Tha steat a tha crops,
An tha price of new hops;
Tha steat a tha nayshun,
An tha leabourers' agitation.
How thay roar an thay laff,
At ache others chaff;
Then goo off an quaff zim mild haff-an-haff.
If thame com yer ta buy, wie wat a quick eye,
Any vaat they'll descry, jist like a Poll Pry;
How tha sheep they'll veel, avore they'll deal,
An ta tha zeller appeal, his price ta reveal,
Zoo an zoo, he'll zay, now I want vor thay,
Nooan better or chaper any money I'll lay.
There beant ta be voun in tha vair groun ta day.
Bit tother ull zay nay, wie accustom'd dismay,
Zich a price I shaant pay,
Zoo I wish ee good day,
An to another lot he'll be off like a shot,
An tha zeam question agen he'll put to tha men
Who stan roun tha pen.

An then he'll propoun,
Can ee warrant em zoun?
While tha men do expoun
Ther qualities roun;
Nooan better ta be voun
In tha vair, they'll be bown.
At las he da buy,
An hoff ull zoon hie,
Tha deal ta ratify,
Be whettin tha eye;
While to zom ragged drover
A trifle's mead over,
To take them to Andover;
Where they mid revel in clover,
On the varm of Jan Glover.

* * * * * *

Of shepperds what a harmy is here,
An ow different zom on em appear;
Zom looks ta av lots a good cheer;
Zom looks main queer an zincere.
Var a minet ta yan stall,
Now jist gie a call;
An teak stock of the company all.
Zee em doin a veed,
Ah, they enjoy it indeed,
Zich appeties wat can exceed;
An tha fare, zee it there.
As much as tha table is yeable ta bear.
A huge jint a zalt beef,
Ya zee head an chief;

Rare stuff, ta gie relief,
Is a shepperds belief.
An yon woppen girt ham,
Wat huge slices they cram ;
Zom voke it hood zicken,
Bit they ate it wie out chicken,
An smack ther lips at tha picken ;
Tripe, an mince meat,
Vaggots, an pigs' veet,
An black puddens stale, on which to regale,
An waish it ael down wie watery ale.

* * * * * *

Now jist take a stride to the other zide, wat a difference wide.
Jist gie a glance at this Restaurance,
As they caal em in Vrance.
If you incline, ya here may dine, of daintees vine,
An waish em down wie sparklin wine.

* * * * * *

'Tis twelve o'clock, an in vull swing is tha Auctioneer's ring
Round his box voke cram, as he baals out ta Zam,
Ta bring in tha vust ram ;
Now gents, wieout any sham, or epigram,
What shall I zay, vor this beautiful ram ?
While the waitin man Zam, hans roun a dram,
Two guineas I hear, in a voice not very clear,
That man he must jeer, or else be in beer ;
He cant be zincere, to offer a price zo queer, vor a ram like this here :

Dree, Vower, Vive, well gents if ya strive,
No doubt you'll contrive, at his vair price ta arrive:
Zix is bid; well, if ever I did;
Look at tha price, he's woth it drice, com be concise, an not za nice: wat a zacrifice.
Zam! to tha bidders roun pass another glass, thay require more brass;
Tha grog an wine da sparkle an shine, an goes down ache line,
Zom decline, bit mwostly incline;
Another spurr, zeven I yer;
Then vrum a woold pate, coms out plump an straite,
Here, I'll gie ee haite, ta en tha debate.
Dally knock un down, zays a countery clown,
An the seller rewards un, wie a terryable vroun.
Then ta nine, another gies tha sign,
Whose eyes da sparkle an shine;
No doubt, effects of tha wine.
Going! going! have ya done? have ya done?
Then roun his quick eyes da run;
Have ya done, wonce again?
Mine I shill not long detain
In pleadings vain;
He looks agen at tha men, who vlock roun tha pen,
Up goes his hand; a voice baals out ten;
An mang ael tha clammer, down goes tha hammer,
An tha lam is zoon hurried out a tha pen,
Ta meak room var another, jist like tha other, one hood think 'twas a brother.
Then ael tha zeam bother is gone droo agen.

*　*　*　*　*　*

If ya've any regard var tha implement yard,
Jist teak a glimpse, but be on yer gard;
Var straps an wheels are continually runnin
An tha naise too is stunnin.
Here be hoers, an mowers, an blowers,
Draigs an jaigs, tha lan ta scarify, and poor vield mice
to terrify.
Mills an drills, elevators and cultevators,
Dressers and pressers, barrers, an larrers, an things ta
ketch sparrers;
Mill stounes an wet stounes.
Rakers and graters, rapers an crapers,
Lifters an zifters, machines for dippin and clippin,
In fact ael things that are out, you zee's laid about,
Ta cultivate lan, by team or by han;
An lots too stan in girt deman,
But raaly var what use I dwoant understan;
Every vair their's zure to be implements newer,
All tha pertickulars of which, you can get vrim vren
Brewer.*
To tha hoss vair advance, an jist gie a glance,
Bit wie girt viligance, var thay rear an thay prance, as
though touched wie a lance,
Especially thay, vrim Erin ar Vrance;
Any zart a steed, you med zee yer indeed,
Any zart a breed, ta jog, ar var speed;
Bit if ya one need, you mist teak girt heed,
An main caushious prozeed, if ya hood zucceed.
Var thease dealers, be zich consalers, an knowin veelers,
An I've yeard tha Peelers, zay zom on em be girt
stalers;

* A local Machinist.

Now jist zee ow ther busines is done,
Jist look at thic poor woold Dun,
Who's wirk vor ever zeems done,
Wat a scare to get un ta run,
How a tries his owner ta shun,
As much as a dog do a gun.
Then look at yon spritely mare,
Brissillen with martial air,
How she gallops wie speed droo tha vair,
While her owner da swear an declare
Zich a gooer never was there ;
Bit if you ud have her, teak care,
Var she medden turn out quite square ;
Zo I'd advise ee, look well, and beware,
Wen ya purchase a hoss at a vair.

* * * * * *

'Tis past mid-day, an they who da stray
Ta every pleace upon tha highway,
Begin ther wares to display ;
Zee yonder Quack begins his clack,
Like a maniac he spouts till he's black ;
Zays he, mines tha tack,
If ya've pains in tha back,
Ar any wur else, I'll cure tha attack ;
Why do ee remain za long in yer pain,
Wen I stoutly maintain
That if you obtain my medicenes plain,
Good health you'll regain, yes ! an retain,
An never agean complain ;

Dwont think ta meak wills,
Bit teak my pills, and be rid of yer ills,
Eece an 'tis zaprisan, wieout disguisin,
Ow many putts vaith in thease Quacks advisin,
Ta thease Quack nex door,
Another vellar da roar.
If ya'm troubled wie a carn,
As true as I'm barn,
Ar a bunyon, or wart, drap two draps on tha part,
An if it dwoant hase impart wieout a paing ar a smart,
I'll ate yon hoss an cart;
On its merrits I wunt dwell,
Var 'tis knaw'd now too well,
Nuthen can it exzell,
It hacks like a spell,
Here! zixpince a bottle I zell.

* * * * * *

Chep Jack begins now to prate,
On his voot bouard a state,
An a crowd a da zoon captivate;
I zay! I zay! I zay!
Good voke jist look this way,
Ya zee I'm cum yer ta day,
Vor I caant stay away;
Now behold my extensive display,
Wich I means ta gie ee ta-day,
That is, var a leetle outlay;
Goods ael new, ya zee on view,
Vrum Brummagem an Lunnen too;

Zo at wonce wieout ado,
Wot vust shill I offer you;
Ah! here's a tay-pot, tha ony one I've got,
Ther beant another in stock,
Tha last of a splendid lot;
Ya zee he's zilver pure,
Of that ya med be zure,
An ya caant one like un procure.
In a zilver smith's shop, I'll be boun,
Var less than a poun,
That is, like thease pure an zoun;
Yer! I shaant zay a poun or a half,
Ah! you med laff an think it chaff;
Yer! *nine, eight, zeven, zix*;
Yer! as true as I'm alive, an in a bit of a fix,
You shell av un var vive,
Ya wunt; very well, I'll putt un by.
Yer! wonce mwoar a gooes var vour,
Yer! hang me, as I'm out on tha spree,
Ya shill av un vor dree;
Yer! two an eleven, two an nine,
Last time, now mine,
Well, as I'm com ta thase town,
Ta get a little renown;
Tho I know I'm done brown,
Zounds, here a gooes var half a crown;
An a knocks un down to a countery clown,
Wie a giggle between a laff an a vrown.
Then his store, he agean do explore,
An brings out wie a roar,
One mbore, jist like the one before.

Now Ballard zingers begin,
Ther charmin verses ta zing,
In anything bit a clear ring ;
Here's well-known Bob an Bet,
Well match'd in ther scramy duet ;
Anuff ta gie ee tha vret,
Tha zouns you'll never varget.
Anyow, ther vaices da charm,
Tha rustic bwoys of tha varm,
Who vlock roun em, likes bees in a swarm ;
An hager ther penny thay pay,
Var tha newest zongs a tha day.

* * * * * *

Here ya ar, as long as thers any,
Vor tha price of one penny ;
Tha newest zongs out, an what they're about ;
Here's "Tha zoldier's joy,"
An "The varmor's bwoy ;"
"A zailer bwold var me,"
"In a cottage be tha sea ;"
"Comin droo tha rye,"
Wie "Tha spider an tha fly ;"
"Belly Maloone,"
"Come, lave I aloone ;"
"Me lads a warrior bwold,"
"Zilver dreads amang tha gwold,"
"Alice Gray," wie "Nellie Ray ;"
"Wilt thou be mine,"
"Tha good Rhine wine ;"

"Auver tha waater,"
Wie "Tha ratcatchers' daater;"
"Out in tha snow,"
"Bit not var Joe;"
"Here stans a pwost,"
"Bill Scroggin's ghost;"
"Cheer bwoys cheer,"
"Vor wie likes a drap a good beer;"
"Brite zunny days," an many mwore lays,
Too numerous ta menshyn,
Ta attract yer attenshin;
An on again, they strike up tha strains,
While tha shepperd's swains,
Join in tha refrains.
Recrutin Zargeants now,
Wie martial brow;
An pleazin bow,
To tha zons of tha plough;
Declare an avow,
That how, thay mist allow;
A zoldiers life, wie tha drum an fife;
An scarlit couat, is one on which to doat;
Com, jine tha line,
Be a zodger vine,
An cut a shine;
Ya'll nevir repent,
Ya did conzent;
Ta teak tha shillin,
Com, ar ya willin;

An many a swain he elevates,
An captivates, be wat he states.

*   *   *   *   *   *

'Tis vower a'clock, an ther's a lull,
Things be getten dull;
Vor wom again,
Is gone tha main,
Be road ar train;
A few remain,
To teak a drain;
Var till next year
Thay wunt meet again.

WOAK APPLE DAY.

A quaint custom, annually kept by the Wishford folks, in order to maintain their rights to the dead and snap wood in Groveley Forest.

Be tha bainks a tha ripplin Wiley,
  Zix mile vrum Zals-bur-ee,
Stans a purty leetle village
  As ever you did zee.

An 'tis yer be zelebrated
  Tha twenty-ninth a May,
A girt big hankshint custom,
  Caal'd girt Woak Apple Day.

Bevore tha zun, on thic ar marń,
  Ar lark, av skim'd tha sky,
Tha village voke be ael astir,
  Shouten ther well know'd cry.

'Tis Groveley; an ael Groveley;
  Com nayburs, lets away,
An keep tha hankshint custom up,
  Var 'tis Woak Apple Day.

Be zix a'clock, a motley crowd
  Av met at Townsend tree,
Bouth woold, an young, var ta keep up
  Thease glad vestivity.

We axe, an hook, away thay goo,
  Ta copse at Groveley,
Ta cut tha woaken boughs out vrom
  Tha merry greenhood tree.

'Tis Groveley; an ael Groveley;
  Tha burden a ther zong,
As ther girt boughs za merrily
  Ache o'm da car along.

An up agean ache cottage dooer,
  Tha woaken bough is tied,
We vlaigs an streamers gay an bright,
  An mottoes too bezide.

'Tis Groveley; an ael Groveley;
  Thame shouten ael tha day,
Ta keep thic hankshint custom up,
  On girt Woak Apple Day.

At one o'clock, thay ael zit down,
  Ta ave a jolly veed,
An 'tis a zite ta cheer yer heart,
  As in country ere wur zeed.

Var ael da zeem zich harminy,
  A gay an happy zene,
We tha ban a playin merrily
  Apon tha village green.

An woold an young, tha rich an poor.
  Join in tha merry dance;
'Tis good ta zee tha upper voke
  Thease pledjures countynance.

Tha Lord a Groveley, he is there,
  An is main plaz'd ta zee,
Tha village voke, enjoy therzelves,
  Thase glad vestivity.

He do respect tha peoples rights,
  Nar wish em var ta barter,
Ther priviliges in Groveley hood,
  Bestow'd on em be Charter.

'Tis Groveley; an ael Groveley;
  A which thay be za proud,
An caas a do respect ther rights
  They cheer un long an loud.

An may em never buse tha right.
  They've got in Groveley hood;
Var 'tis a girt boon to tha poor,
  Granted ta do em good.

* * * * *

An zoo let's cheer, Lord Pembroke long,
  Likewise tha Girt woak tree;
An ael tha Wishford voke who've got
  Thease rights in Groveley.

'Tis Groveley; an ael Groveley;
  Tha burden a ther Charter,
An never med thease village voke
  Ther hankshint rights ere barter.

OWER GOOD WOLD PASSIN.

O, ad I jist tha power ta rite,
Like Bob Burns, vor a zingle nite,
I hood zit down, we ael me mite,
  An praize ower good wold Passin.

Vor zirch tha countery ael aroun,
A better one ther caant be voun,
That in good works da zo aboun,
  As ower good wold Passin.

He is a good un, every ninch,
Vrum nuthun good he'll never vlinch,
An'll never zee wie poor voke pinch,
  Will ower good wold Passin.

When zickness hunts tha poor man's cot,
An empty runs his shelf an pot,
Who is it cheers his lowly lot?
  Why, ower good wold Passin.

Who, when he's on a bade a pain,
Do we good things his straingth zustain,
An offen droo tha nite remain?
  Why, ower good wold Passin.

Who, wen tha han a death comes down,
An zens zich gloom on ael aroun,
Who is it trys tha grief ta droun
  Why, ower good wold Passin.

Who helps tha widder in hur grief,
Who in pity ant got no belief,
Bit in gien out stanchill relief?
  Why our good wold Passin.

Who's always vull a readiness,
Ta teak tha children vatherless,
An zee em brought ta usevulness?
  Why, ower good wold Passin.

Who gets tha maids wie rozy feazin,
Out in tha wordle tha best a plazin,
Who ther deeds is alwys prazin?
  Why, ower good wold Passin.

Who ta that girt house aft ull goo,
Var aid ta help his good wirk droo,
  'tis mwore than his means ull do?
  Why, ower good wold Passin.

Who, wie tha Squire aft ull plead,
Tha kease of zom poor bwoy in need,
That vor'un he med intercede?
  Why, ower good wold Passin.

Who, wen Varmers an ther men vaals out,
Tha leabourers' cause gets up an spout,
An bring agean zweet pace about?
  Why, ower good wold Passin.

Who, when tha Winter's cwold an sharp,
Zens out we coals his hoss an cart,
To tha wold voke zo's thay shaant smart?
  Why, ower good wold Passin.

Who, wen merry Crismiss comes aroun,
At every poor man's cot is voun,
Gien every head, prime beef a poun,
  Why, ower good wold Passin.

No poor man never he'll refuse,
Tho he dwoant vaal in wie his views;
Ar if ta meetin house a gooes,
  Dwoant matter ta ower wold Passin.

A, zirch tha Countery ael about,
A better man ya wunt vind out,
Zo his praise vor ever I ull shout,
  Cos he's a downrite good wold Passin.

GRAMFER SHAANT GOO INTA WIRKHOUSE.

Nunno! a shaant goo inta Wirkhouse
  While I've a crowst a bread,
An can manage var ta keep
  A roof auver me yead.

As long as I have got me health,
  An straingth ta yarn a shillin,
An tha parish voke ull low a bit,
  Ta keep un I be willin.

An if tha wunt, I'd zooner pinch
  Than zee un goo up there,
Aelthough 'tis baddish times anuff,
  An nuthen I've ta speare.

Var poor woold man he's haighty two,
  His hair's as white as snow,
An totterin is his gait an step,
  A da sheak an trimble zo.

Mworn zixty years a shepperdin
  A wur apon tha plaain,
As bwoy, an man, a tenden sheep
  I wind an starm and rain.

An many be tha zites he've zeed,
  An many be tha tales,
What happen'd when a wur a bwoy,
  Amang thease hills an vales.

When I, a chile, how many times
  He've took I on his knee,
An twould I bout girt Wellinton,
  An his veamous victory.

An tears thay hood rin out his eyes,
  As thic tale he went droo,
Var his ony bwoy : my Fiather brave,
  Wur killed at Waterloo.

Eece, an well he caals ta mine tha day
  When tha steage coach did rattle
We lightenin speed ael droo thease vale
  We news of thic girt battle.

How, when a stopped a leetle while
  At tha public on tha green,
Tha village voke ael vlock'd aroun
  To hear tha news za keen.

And when twur know'd that Wellinton,
  Had konkerd Bonnypart,
What cheers went up, za long, an loud,
  Vrim every English heart.

Var droo tha country Bonny's neam
  Had caas'd voke girt alarm,
An down right thankvull wur em now
  A cooden do no yarm.

An long tha thankvull cheers went up,
  An drink went vreely round,
We jay, becaas tha English voke
  Had beat the Vrenchmin zound.

Nevir avore, an nevir zunce,
  Av ther bin zich adoo,
Ael droo tha lan, as when tha news
  Did com bout Waterloo.

Var twur a glorious vite, da zaay,
  Woold zawljers, brave an hoary,
Who's livin now ta tell about
  Thic ar veam'd day a glory.

Bit when tha vlush a victory
  Had passed away again,
What mwournen did goo droo tha lan
  Var thousands that wur slain.

An when tha news rach'd Gramfer's cot
  That Fiather he wur kill'd,
What tears wur shed, what anguish keen
  Mother an Gramfer vill'd.

Bit nevir mind me lass, zaays he,
  A Fiather now I'll be,
Thy mate, my zon, died viten vur
  His king and countery.

Tha widder an tha vatherless
  A took into his cot,
An well a keer'd var bouath a we,
  Till I ta manhood got.

An shill I then, now he is woold,
  Not yeable var ta wirk,
Ze un goo hoff ta Wirkhouse,
  An me bounden duty shirk.

Nunno, a shaant goo inta Wirkhouse,
  Bit com an sheare me cot,
Tho' main scanty be me means,
  A shill have haf I got.

Var poor woold man he's helpless quite
  An veeble as a chile,
His wants be vew, his heart's content,
  Var ael he've got a smile.

An shood er live a vew mwore years,
  I'll do my baste ta cheer
An brighten up his days a bit,
  As long as he be here.

In zummer, wen tha days be warm.
  In archet he shill perch,
Under tha girt elm tree an watch
  Tha voke goo inta Church.

An when tha evenins thay be vine,
  I'll vill his heart wie jay,
An teak un out amang tha zenes,
  A rambled, wen a bwoy.

I'll draa un out on top tha hill,
  In Squire's dree-wheel'd cheer,
Zo's he can look aroun wonce mwore
  On zenes that be za dear.

An wen tha gloomy winter comes,
  An vrost an snow be here,
He shill zit warm an cozy like,
  In his girt big yarm cheer.

An while tha log is burnin bright,
  Agean he shall goo droo,
His oft twould tale a Wellinton
  An tha vite at Waterloo.

Zoo a shaant goo inta Wirkhouse,
  While I've a crowst a bread,
An can manage var ta keep
  A roof auver me yead.

GRAMFER'S CRISMIS.

Eece ! Crismis in me gramfer's time,
  Wur a proper zart a randy,
Var he invited ael tha voke
  As liv'd aroun un, handy,

Uncles, an aunts, an cuzzens too,
  Nevvys an nieces vair,
A did invite em every one
  Ta teast his Crismis vare.

Twur ael tha taak var many a day,
  Wur gramfer's Crismis pearty ;
Amang the people who went up,
  Ta greet the woold man hearty.

Var ael wur equal in his eyes
  When zated at his bouard,
An narn o'm never hood er slight,
  Tho much, thay cooden avoord.

A proper good woold zart wur he,
An lov'd be rich an poor,
I warn, nar ungry man eer went,
Away vrim gramfer's door.

On Crismis Eve, tha woold varm house
Wur trimmed up high an low,
Wie evergreens an hollies bright,
An boughs a mizzletoe.

An vrim tha kitchen, ael the things
Wur clared out var a ball;
An ony cheers an stools wur left,
Var sates aroun tha wall.

A blazin vire wur mead up,
Apon tha kitchen dogs;
An gramfer's varm men did bring in,
Tha girt big Crismis logs.

At haight a clock tha Mummers come,
Ten a tha village chaps,
Dressed up as zowljers, bright an gay,
We girt tall peapern caps.

An hooden zwoords mwoast ad a got:
One we a blunderbuss;
An Fiather Crismis car'd a staff:
Man Jack, tha money puss.

An thay did act a girt long piece,
An a battle tend ta vite;
An run hache other droo tha hearts,
Wich mead the maids turn white.

Bit tha chap as acted doctor,
  Zoon rais'd em vrim the ground,
An quick, we a drap a brandy,
  Very zoon did bring em round.

An atter every man o'm there,
  Had bin wounded in tha vray;
Thay ael begun tá zing za nice,
  Tha ditties a tha day.

Then Fiather Crismis mead a spache,
  A wishen ael good cheer;
Likewise a merry Crismis tide,
  An happy bright new year.

An atter that, thay ate an drunk,
  As much as thay wur willin;
Then out comes grammer, an she gies
  Ta every man a shillin.

An leetle Jack we's money baig,
  Went roun tha company;
An lots a pennies wur drow'd in,
  Var's own zelf, dwoant ee zee.

At midnight then did come tha Waits,
  Ower village music pearty;
An thay het up ther praizes sweet,
  A Crismis carols hearty.

Two viddles, an a double bease,
  Two brassen things ta blow;
We maids ta zing the hayre high,
  An men ta zing down low.

An thay did play an zing za sweet,
Round gramfer's kitchen vire;
While grammer quarts a gin hot brew'd,
A wich thay diden tire.

Zides that, a goolden guinea bright,
Woold gramfer ne'er vargot.
Ta gie ta em, avore they went,
Ta sheare amang tha lot.

On Crismis marn, then down ta chirch,
Tha varm house pearty went,
Ta thank God var thease blessed day,
Tha heavenly Beabe wur zent.

An lore! ta hear tha zingin bright,
Girt tears a joy did bring,
Down gramfer's an down grammer's cheeks,
Praizen tha New born King.

Var thay wur times, when good chirch voke,
Ther praises zung tagether;
Tha choir wur bit ta lead em on,
Noo zarplices ta zever.

Ah eece, thame zounds I hant vargot,
Still in me ears da ring,
Thic well know'd tune, "While Shepperds Watch"
An "Hark the Angels zing."

Then ael tha company atter chirch,
Ta gramfer's did repair;
Ta zit down in his speacious hall,
An enjoy his Crismis vare.

Varty ar fifty voke there wur,
  Countin tha young an woold;
A twur a zite, thic vestive bouard,
  Var a body to behold.

Var at tha top, a piece a beef
  Bout vive an thirty poun;
Zides hams an two girt turkeys vat,
  Done up za nice an brown.

An vlow'ry teaties beak'd an bwil'd,
  Pasmets an carrits too;
Cabbidge an smaish'd per turmets white,
  In piles ther wur ta view.

Figgetty poodens roun an plump,
  As bigs a waishen pot;
Mince pies an tearts a every zart,
  Lore! wurden there a lot.

An yale an zider, in quart mugs,
  Wur putted here an there.
Var hache ta help therzelves wen dry,
  An waish down the wholzum vare.

An lore! ta zee how hearty like,
  Hache let in we his might,
Ta tackle gramfer's Crismis cheer,
  Var mworn a nower quite.

Wen everyone had had ther vill,
  Tha cloth wur clar'd away,
An roun ael zat be vire za bright,
  Za happy like an gay.

Then out comes grammer's wom mead wine,
  Sparklin, an bright's a cherry ;
Wich in harnen cups wur handed roun :
  Rare stuff ta meak ee merry.

An trays a nice ripe oranges,
  We apples russet brown ;
An hazzel nuts an walnuts too,
  Wich last vall wur shook down.

An gramfer he drunk'd ael ower healths,
  A wur glad ta zee ess there,
An hoped a shood as long as heav'n
  His life wur plaz'd ta spare.

An then tha men voke every one,
  We feazin rid an happy,
Went out in kitchen var ta av
  A leetle bit a baccy.

We young uns, an tha coortin voke,
  Went out ta av a run,
In archit ar in gramfer's vields,
  Var a leetle bit a vun.

An if twur vrosty weather, we,
  Down pond did meak a slide ;
An jine han's on tha glassen vloor,
  An nice along did glide.

Ar if tha snow wur thic on groun,
  We ael zet up snow ballin ;
An twur rare vun ta hear tha maids,
  A screechen an a squallen.

An wen twur dark, back to tha varm,
  We purty zoon did hie;
Ta tittyvate ourzelves a bit,
  Var tha girt ball bime by.

At haight a clock tha dance begun,
  Out in tha kitchen wide;
Tha musickers, they wur perch'd up,
  On a teable tother zide.

There wur viddler Joe, an carnet Jack,
  An Steve wie his pum, pum,
An Zammy we tha double bease,
  An Jim ta beat tha drum.

Vull twenty couple did stan up,
  In tha vust country dance;
Led off be gramfer an his deam,
  Lore! how we ael did prance.

Vull haaf a nower we kep on,
  Gwain up an down the middle,
Till nearly ael tha ban gied out,
  Cept Joe, wie leaden viddle.

Bit he kep on a screapen zo,
  Till ower laigs begun ta yeak;
An grammer then she did baal out,
  "Do'ee stop var goodness seak."

Then gramfer he did zing a zong,
  Bout days, A woold lang syne;
An in chorus, everybiddy there,
  Mwoast heartily did jine.

An grammer, too, we wirk'd her up,
  Ta zing a leetle ditty;
An var a lass a zeventy two,
  Her voice wur strong an purty.

A geam a varvits then we had,
  Ael zit down in a row;
An they as lost had to be kiss'd,
  Under tha mizzletoe.

Zoo, we dancin an wie zingin too,
  Away tha hours did vlee,
An wen twur twelve, tha ban struck up,
  Roger de Coverley.

An hache pair danc'd ael down tha line
  Wie feazin ael aglow,
Tha young men kiss'd their pierdeners
  Under tha mizzletoe.

Tha woold uns too, then vollied zuit
  An kiss'd ache other too,
Thay wurden gwain ta be done out
  A what thay used ta do.

Var gramfer kiss'd tha maidens sweet,
  An grammer kiss'd tha bwoys,
Lar, what a fectin zite it wur
  Amang tha vun an naise,

At one a clock, tha ban begun
  Ta play "God seave tha King,"
An fifty voices purty zoon,
  Mead thic woold roof tree ring.

Then com varewells, an sheakin hans,
  Tho ael wur louth ta peart;
An as thay went thay loud did cheer,
  Gramfer, we ael their heart.

* * * * * *

An thus did gramfer every year,
  Ax vrens ta dine an zup;
An med I live ta do the zeam,
  An keep woold Crismis up.

GOOD VRIDY LAS.

Good Vridy las, as ever wur,
  I wander'd to tha hood ;
Tha joyous spring birds var ta hear,
  An sniff tha air za good.

Droo Ugvird vale, I took me way,
  An out in broad Ox drove,
Wur many times when young an gay,
  I rambled wie me love.

Athirt tha cloas cropt'd down I went,
  An zat down be tha pond ;
A blissvul nower there I spent,
  Gazin on things za vond.

Woold Vriars Pake ; there on me lift,
  In vront, tha thymy down
Behine ; tha copse of hazzel trees
  Wur nuts da grow za brown.

What thoughts da come across I here,
  A long, long, years agoo,
Wen a bwoy, as now, I did delight
  Thease zenes ta wander droo.

Var every hallerdy amwoast,
We merry bwoys wur voun,
We bat an ball, ower rounders play
Apon thease open down.

Agean I jogged on auver hill,
An cross tha Barvird track,
Then down ta Chilvinch bottom, still,
Cloas to tha narrer rack.

It wur a glorious atternoon,
An hot, var hearly spring,
Jist like a day in balmy June,
Zoo gay wur everything.

Tha bumble bees, begun ta buzz,
Tha knats ta sting an bite,
An out amang yan bloomin vuzz,
Buttervlies vlitted bright.

Rabbits, an hares, vrim copse, za shy,
Wur skippin vree an wild,
An patridges, who's screechin cry
Is know'd be every child.

Vrum vield, an down, tha lark went up
Ta welcome in tha spring,
Tha merry blackbird, an tha drush,
Did meak tha woodland ring,

An vrim a low branch of yon woak
Tha timid nightengale
Had jist begun ta tune his voice
An trill his artless tale.

An here between tha moss an thyme,
  Wild violets wur a blowin,
An primroses, in ael their prime,
  Wie cowzlips jist a showin.

Mid zich an unzurpassin zene,
  As this in thease sweet dell,
Me heart delights, an here I cood
  Var ever zeem ta dwell.

Then up a well wor'd track I stroll'd,
  Towards a beech hard bye,
Apon who's trunk, there is carv'd out,
  Zim letters dear ta I.

Here, mwore an thirty years agone,
  Wie a zweet modest lass,
Thic tree ower neames I carv'd apon,
  Love's idle nower ta pass.

An here ta day, they letters still,
  Be showin out za plain ;
Ah ! what girt thoughts me heart da vill
  As I zees em again.

Var cars me back ta youthvul days,
  When I, za gay an vree,
Did taak a love, an breathe sweet zighs,
  Under thease woold beech tree.

Jist twenty zummers had I zeed,
  Thic ne'er vargotten day,
Tha time a my apprenticship
  Had nearly pass'd away.

An vull a hope, me heart beat high,
  Var a zuccessvul life,
An com what hood, I'd bwoldly try,
  Ta veace thease wordles strife.

An zunce thic day, what zenes I've zeed,
  What trials I've a bore,
What crosses, an what ups and downs,
  An many draabacks zore.

Teant mine ta bwoast, teant mine ta braig,
  A honner ar a wealth,
Bit a crowst, I've never wanted var,
  An God av gied I health.

An atter ael thease thirty years,
  Strivin ta do me best,
In gratitude I drap a tear,
  Var zure I have bin blest.

Tho well I knaw, I have vill shart
  A what I ought ta done,
Heet hard I've striv'd ta do me peart,
  Tho tis a humble one.

HAYMEAKIN ZONG.

When Midzummer is draain nigh,
An grass in mead an vield is high;
Up we tha zun away da go,
Tha mawers var ta lay it low;
Wie gleamin sythe thay ael tha day,
Da whet, an swet, an mow away;
While wives da vollie on behind,
An sheak tha swaths out to tha wind.

CHORUS.

Var haymeakin in zummer prime,
Is a joyvul happy time.

Them strappen chaps, Jim, Jack, an Joe,
Be rare good fellers var ta mow;
Auver a yeaker in a day,
Thay'll cut, an caal it purty play;
An zomtimes thay ull av a bout,
Ta zee who vust on em gies out;
Bit Joe's tha baste man a tha dree,
Ther's narn ta come up zides we he.

Var haymeakin, &c.

Down mead, it be a purty zite,
When tha weather's warm and bright;
Ta hear tha glad haymeakin voke,
Za merry like we zong an joke;
Ta zee tha childern jump an play,
An rompse amang tha new mown hay;
An coortin couples be tha brook,
Wanderen to zom sheady nook.

Var haymeakin, &c.

Measter an Missus oft comes out,
Ta help an turn tha hay about;
Ther strappen zon, an daaters gay,
Likes ta vrolic we tha hay;
Var plazes em ta zee tha cut,
An smill tha scent as sweets a nut;
An oft, ull zend var extry beer,
Tha leaberen people var ta cheer.

Var haymeakin, &c.

At nunchin time, vrom tha hot zun,
Ta yander willer tree thay run,
Which by tha river's baink da spread;
Like a girt tent up auver yead,
An here tha zimple vare gooes down,
A braden cheese, an yale za brown,
Which every man, ooman an bwoy,
Hearty an happy do enjoy.

Var haymeakin, &c.

An when tha grass is ael cut down,
An zun an wind av dried it brown,
Hosses an waiggins purty quick,
Haals it away up ta tha rick ;
An when tis zeafly inta stack,
Beeans an Beakin is tha tack ;
Girt poodens too, baccy an beer,
An close tha day we jolly cheer.

Var haymeakin in zummer prime,
Is a joyvul happy time.

HARVUST WOM SONG.

Tune—"*Auld Lang Syne.*"

Good harvust chaps as handy lives,
  Ta thase yer leetle town;
Com stir yerzelves about ta keep;
  Thease day a girt renown;
Var 'tis tha day of ael tha year,
  When men an measters vree;
Tagether shall enjoy therzelves,
  In parfect unity.

CHORUS :—

Let love an vrenship on thease day,
  Ael evils auvercom;
An wie good cheer, a beef an beer,
  We'll keep our harvust wom.

Com wives an daaters that av help'd
  Ta get tha harvust in ;
Com putt yer bran new dresses on,
  Ta liven up tha zene.
Com Moll, an Doll, an Poll, an Zue,
  Com Vanny an Marier ;
An every one that wirks about,
  Var Hirl ar var Squire.
    Let love an vrenship on thease day, &c.

To church we vust of ael ull goo,
  In a girt raink za gran ;
A marchin jist like zodgers bwold,
  Ta tha tune of ower brass ban ;
An there ower thanks we will pour out,
  Ta He who lives on hi ;
Var ael tha goods things he da zen,
  Ower mouths ta zatisfy.
    Let love an vrenship on thease day, &c.

Ta measter's house then back we'll goo,
  Wie shearpened appetite ;
An zoon at girt big spicy jints,
  Let in wie ael ower mite ;
An ater that we'll smoke an zing,
  An measter's healths we'll drink ;
While young uns thay shill dance away,
  Till ther eyes begin ta blink.

    Let love an vrenship on thease day,
      Ael evils auvercom ;
    An wie good cheer, a beef an beer,
      We'll keep our harvust wom.

THA LEABOURER'S ZUNDY MARNIN.

Eece, Zundy marn in zummer prime
Ta tha leabourer is a appy time,
It is tha day that he likes baste,
Var he can zit un down an raste,
An think apon tha things above,
An meditate on heaven's love.
Then wen tha zun is risin high
Up in tha girt big cloudless sky,
On Zundy marnin out a gooes
Ta let tha cows an hosses loose,
An teak om ta tha vlowry mead,
Wur thay ael day in pace can veed.
Zee ow tha poor things pranks about,
Var well thay knaas thay be let out,
An be their looks thay zeems ta zay—
"No wirk is there var we ta day;"
An man is thankvul unto heaven
That there is mead one day in zeven
That animals as well as he
Can raste vrim toil and be vree.

Tha good man then meaks vast tha geat,
An on its bars a takes a zeat,
An wie a innerd joy pervound,
Smilin, looks out on ael around ;
He zees tha curlin smoke arise
Vrim his cottage chimley ta tha skies,
Wur busy wife we cheervul zmile
Da blow ta meak tha kiddle bwile.
He hears tha rooks a caain, high
Up in tha elems stannin by,
Mingled wie tha sheep bells zouns
Away vrim off tha upland downs,
An larks a whirrlin too on high
Their marnin carols to tha sky,
Tha blackbird sweet and merry drush
Zingin away in yander bush,
An tha cuckoo's well know'd cry
In tha big archet handy bye,
Wie tha peweets wailin scream,
An mwournens vlutter in tha stream,
Wur speckled trout, we watchvul eye,
Springs up ta ketch tha heedles vly,
An merry milk bwoy on his way
Ta deairy, hums a zacred lay.
An every thing zeems thankin heaven
Var thease one blessed day in zeven.
An now he hears tha woold church bell
Tinklin zlowly in tha dell,
An its woold vamiliar chime
Tells un that tis breakfist time ;

Then zlowly back he da retreat,
An leetle childern run ta meet
Ther dad we many a plazin smile,
Which da tha good man's heart beguile;
Tha youngest on his back a takes,
Then to his cot his way he makes.

To tha leabourer how zweet it is
That he can greet one day as his;
Var ah, wat pledure he da veel,
Wen zated at tha marnin meal.
Ta zee his childern in their place.
An hear em zing aloud tha grace;
Zo different to a wirken day,
Wen he must needs be vur away
Early an late at weary toil,
Ta cultivate tha rugged zoil;
Vrom Mondy marn till Zaturday,
No chaance he has ta tak ta thay.
Zo now a meakes good use a time.
An rades an taks till church bells chime;
An off tha good man then da go,
Wie his dree childern in a row,
Away down ta tha village church,
An greets tha zexton in tha porch,
Var tis his fiather, aged man,
That teaks tha childern be tha han,
An leads em roun tha church yard green,
Ta where a leetle mound is zeen,
Covered we vlowers in vull blow,
Tha grave of his dear wife below;

Tha woold man draps a fervent tear,
An zays "me leetle childern dear,
Here lies yer granny, kine woold heart,
Who here on earth did well her peart.
Now teak a rose me childern dree,
Emblems var you ta think on she.
Var ye be vlowers now on earth,
An vull a joy, an health, an mirth;
Bit woold age ull com, you'll vade away,
An like yer granny, zoo you'll lay."
Thus nearly every Zundy marnin
Tha woold man gie'd tha childern warnen,
Wen thay did goo tha church yard round,
Ta zee ther granny's leetle mound.

An now tha woold church bells have done,
Tha mornin zarvice is begun;
Tha congregation, modestly,
Rades an responds mwoast reverently;
An choir, up in tha gallery,
Da play an zing mwoast heartily;
Ael zarts a insterments are there.
We childern's voices high in air,
An earnestly, wie zolemn face,
Men in white smocks a zingen bass.
O you who lives in polished towns,
Who be za used ta viner zouns,
Dwoant ee look down we cool disdain,
Upon thease choristers za plaain;
Var tho ther med be zom discord,
Heaven doth ther yarnest praise regard.

Tha passon in his desk da rade,
An tha psalms a David lade
He prays an praches yarnestly,
An taks of Heaven joyously;
Wur ael that zarve tha Lord arright
Will shine we lustre sparklin bright;
Wur ael is happiness provound,
An purity da reign around;
Wur every biddys vree vrim stain,
An pure equality da reign;
Wur toil an hardship cease ta be,
An tha poor leabourer is vree;
Wur ael is pace, an love, an joy,
An praises do tha tongue employ;
Wur tha Lamb zits on tha throne,
Who var poor zinners do atone;
An we wat a holy smile He
Is sated in girt Majesty;
Ther Ho da zit an bid ess com
Ta his eternal blessed wom.
An thus tha good man do appeal,
An many a zilent tear ull steal
Ael down tha leabourer's burly veace,
Ta know var he that there is greace;
An tears like thase be prayers breave'd
Var thay as cannot words conceive;
Tho zometimes shed wie zorroin moan,
Thay zure be witnessed vrim tha throne.
An meekly now ael bow the yead,
While tha last benediction's zaid.

Tha marnin zarvice now is o'er,
Wie zolemn step a laves tha door;
Wie childern, seeks agean his cot,
An thinks how happy is his lot;
While busy wife da quick prepare
Tha Sabbath meal of humble fare;
A piece of bwiled beakon hot,
An vegetables vrim gierden plot;
An zuety dumplins, roun an plump,
Which meaks tha hager childern jump.
Ta tha leabourer tis indeed a treat
That he zich vare as this can greet;
Var on wirken days out in tha viel,
On brade an cheese he makes his meal.
An who shall say these voke be zinners
Ta zit down to cook'd Zundy dinners.

* * * * * *

An now, wie zolemn up turned veace,
Tha childern zing aloud their greace;
Ax var a blessin on tha vood,
Ta da their zouls and bodies good.
An in quick time, a never vear,
Tha good things provided disappear;
Thay once agean gies thanks ta heaven,
Var ael tha marcies God hath given.
An sweet contentment vills their cot,
Thay'm happy, an thay murmer not.
Ay! much above tha wordle's scornnen
Is tha leabourer's cot on Zundy marnin.

THA SNOW.

Tha snow, tha snow, is vallen,
An my good deam, she be callen,
"Be quick, good man, hie out a tha starm,
An com to yer snug leetle cottage, za warm."

Tha snow, tha snow, ael droo tha snow,
Away to his wirk tha poor man mist go;
Bit, ah, wen at nite a greets his snug cot,
An smills his hot zupper, his keers be vargot.

When tha snow lays deep and vrosts da bite,
An tha vields an downs be covered quite,
Tha leabourer sturdy, up in the vield barn,
Be-leabours ael day tha russet brown carn.

Tha vrost an tha snow tho cheerless they zeems,
Tha zweets that thay avs ther roughness redeems;
Var where will ee vine a cozier zite
Than a leabourer's cot on a cwould winter's nite.

THA CARTER'S WINTER ZONG.

Tha leaves be turnin yaller,
  Cwold winds begin ta blow,
An zoon Jan vrost u'll com along
  An bring ess ice an snow.
But let un com, we dwoant dislike
  Ta zee his feace at ael,
Vor droo tha nites of winter cwold
  We keeps high vestival.

CHORUS.

Vor roun tha blazin kitchen vire
  We drink an smoke away,
We tell ower tales, an zing ower zongs,
  An kiss tha maidens gay.

At nite, ow nice ta lay in bade
  An hear tha storm outzide,
An shrug yer showders at tha zound,
  An wish ya there cud bide.
But offen we outzide mist be
  Apon tha wintry road,
But then we knows wat jay twill be
  Wen we gets wom our load.

Vor roun the blazin kitchen vire, &c.

Ta get up of a winter's marn
An zee snaw on tha groun,
It raaly is a purty zite
Ta zee it ael aroun,
Ta zee tha girt big flakes za white
Za thick up in tha air,
Ta vind tha ponds ael vrozen up
An everything za bare.

Vor roun tha blazen kitchen vire, &c.

Then in tha barn, zich times as thease,
We likes ta dresh ael day,
Vor warm an jolly we da get
Jist zo twur zummer gay.
Let winter be as sharp as t'will,
Right jolly chaps be we;
Vor glad delight we avs at nite,
Za merry an za vree.

Vor roun tha blazin kitchen vire
We drink an smoke away,
We zing ower zongs, an kiss tha maids,
We jolly carters gay.

THA PUZZLED VOTER.

A DIALOGUE BETWEEN HUSBAN AN WIFE.

Husban just come in vrim Work.

WIFE.

"Why Bob! who's think bin yer ta-day?"

HUSBAN.

"Well, raly Polly, I ca'ant zay."

WIFE.

"Why Squire Jinkins an he's daater,
As da live down at Blackwater."

HUSBAN.

"Well, and what do em want a we?
Teant oft poor voke thay comes ta zee."

WIFE.

"Thats true Bob; I'll tell ee presently,
What var thay come ta visit we.
Doo'st know? a Lections purty near,
An thay da want yer vote, me dear.
Thay ax'd if you wur Red ar Blue,
Be drat if I did know, thats true,

Pollyticks, thay diden trouble you,
Ya diden keer var Red nar Blue.
At that tha Squire rais'd his peepers
An zays: 'what! dwoant er rade tha peapers,
Ta zee whats done in Parleyment,
Be gennelmen who there be zent?'
O eece, I zays: 'Bob rades tha news,
Bit twixt em, there yeant much ta choose.
He zays, bouth zides in pollyticks
Cars on a lot a artvul tricks,
Bouath on ems tar'd we tha seam brush,
An ta wirkin voke beant woth a rush.
Zoo raly, I caant tell ee, Squire,
Which on em Bob da mwoastly mire.'"

HUSBAN.

"Well Poll, tis right what you've a zed,
I beant a Blue, nar neet a Red,
Becos, as vur as I can zee,
Narn on em beant no good ta we.
'Tis job ta tell which o'm vrim tother,
Thay'm bout as bad as one another;
Thay bouath da promise this an that,
But tis a lot a bosh, thats pat,
Var when thay gets in Parleyment,
Their mines on other things be bent,
An thay vargets when thame up there,
Ael there nice promises za vair.
As var meakin laas, var we poor voke,
Till ael goo off in empty smoke."

" Well Bob, Squire zays tha Blues be right,
An var we poor da aelways fight,
Zoo I twould'n straite if that wur true
I'd zee my Bob shood vote var Blue.
Madam a zays, 'tis zartin vacts;
Jist rade yerzelf tha many acts
That they've a pass'd var ael tha poor,
An blessins brought ta every door.'
Thease gran woold Englin he did zay,
Wur neer in zich a prosperous way,
You, as a wirkin man's good wife,
Wur never better off in yer life.
Brade is chep, an groceries too,
Var ael this you must thank tha Blue;
Agean, jist look and zee, he zays
Tha good thay've done in many ways,
If yer husban ony looks ta zee,
What benefits thay've done var he.
If be accident, a now gets hurt,
An meets wie mishap at his wirk,
His employer he'll have ta pay
His wages, long as he's away.
Yeant that, yer grievances redressin?
An to ache wirkin man a blessin?"

* * * * *

Coose Bob, I cooden well deny
Ael that tha Squire zed ta I.
" Zoo then I ax'd un bout thase war,
An what ower voke wur vi'tin var?

A zed, bout twenty yer agoo,
We tha Boers we had a fillyloo,
An at a place caal'd Juber Hill
A regiment nearly thay did kill;
Gladstin, who wur in power then,
Insteeds a zendin out mwore men
Vargeed em, and ever zunce thic day,
Thay've bused our voke in every way,
And swear'd that every Britisher,
Thay'd zoon drave out a Africker;
An coose we had ta let em know
Jan Bull a hood'nt be trated so.

* * * * *

O well I zed, if that be true
I'll zee my Bob shill vote var Blue.

* * * * *

Zoo in a book he mead a note,
As Robert Spencer, Blue, hood vote."

HUSBAN.

"Well Poll, ya shooden twould un that,
I dwoant knaa now what to be at,
Var's I wur comin wom ta-night,
Who shid I zee bit Captin Wright,
A passen in he's hoss and trap;
A zays, 'Well Bob, you'm jist tha chap,
As I'm a draven out ta zee,
I wants a leetle chat we ee;
I'm putten up var Parleyment,
An hopes as how ya will conzent,
Ta vote var I on pollen day,
An that you will, me vren, now zay.

We Reds, be ael vor wirkin men,
An'll do well vor em you may depen,
An nuthen shill thase course prevent,
When we da get in Parleyment.
Zee, what tha peartys done var you!
An their good Acts, jist rim em droo!
We Reds, tha corn laas did repeal,
An now, poor men can av a meal
A braden mate, ar braden cheese,
When vore their bellies thay mist squeeze,
An barley bannicks live apon.
That's zartin true upon me zong,
Tha Reds bin wirkin ael their life
Var tha poor leabourer and he's wife.'

* * * * *

If thats zoo Captin out I zed,
Be drat if I dwoant vote var Red.
An then I menshind bout tha war,
An what ower voke wur vi'tin var?
I zays, tha Boers be a rum lot,
An zars em right jist what they've got.
Var's I da rade tha truth on't wur.
Thay dreaten'd we in Africker,
If we diden gree wieout delay!
Purty quick thay'd drave ess in tha sae,
I hopes if I da vote var you,
Zich bwoastin you'll meak em rue,
An never trust to em agen,
To rule auver any Englishmen."

" An what did Captin zay ta that?
I'm glad ya putt it to un pat,
Cos Squire zed tha Lib'rils zure
Nearly ael zided we tha Boer."

HUSBAN.

" O no a zays, tha Boers agen
Ull never rule o'er Englishmen,
Their geam is up, thay mist zit down
In pace under tha British crown.
Although tha Reds be geanst tha Blues,
We mwoastly holds imperial views ;
An now tha Boers be konker'd quite,
We Reds ull zoon meak things ael right.
If this be zo ; then Captin Wright,
I promise ee my vote thease night :
An vaithvul stick ta what I've zed,
On pollen day be voten Red.

*   *   *   *   *

Then in he's book he mead a note
As Robert Spenser, Red, hood vote."

WIFE.

" Well Bob, we'm in a purty stew !
I promis'd Squire ya shoud vote Blue ;
He's zich a nice man, an young Miss
Avore she went gied Beab a kiss ;
An zed she purty zoon did mean,
Ta come an zee ess ael agean.

Var my zeak Bob, I hopes as you,
On pollen day ull vote var Blue ;
An if you'll ony promise this,
I'll gie ee zich a l'ovin kiss ;
An praps Miss Jinkins she med too,
No knowen what she medden do.
Now zay you will ; now there's a dear ;
Bout Captin Wright ya need'n vear.

HUSBAN.

" Why Poll ya do get auver I,
Var what ya ax, who can deny ;
Thay eyes a yourn, da pierce I droo,
Anything amwoast thay'll meak I do.
Bit dang it, what ull Captin zay ?
If I votes Blue on pollen day."

WIFE.

Why he wunt knaa, ya zilly elf,
Unless ya tell's un zo yerzelf ;
Tha votens done in sacrit now,
No one ull vind it out, I vow."

HUSBAN.

" Ael right me dear, anuffs bin zed,
I'm tired out, an longs var bed ;
When there, praps I med drame a bit
How to get out a thase yer clit.

* * * * *

Pollen day. Husban just returned.

WIFE.

" Well now dear Bob, now tell I true,
Did'ee ar didn'ee vote var Blue

Come zay, an zet me mine at rest,
I'll keep it sacrit in me breast.
No biddys about, and nooan'll hear.
Now do ee tell I, there's a dear."

HUSBAN.

"Well Poll, I do believe ya'd draa
A sacrit out a ower Jack Daa.
Well then, jist hear how I did vote,
An mine on it teak proper note:
Twix Reds and Blues, tid beat tha Devil!
Ta vind who's right; I mead em level:
At bouath o'ms neam, I put a cross,
An zoo var I, thame Hoss, and Hoss,
As we da zay in skiddle alley,
When tha scorin it da tally.
Zoo if Squire he da caal on we,
Tell un I mead a cross war he.
An if Captin should tha subject neam,
I'll zay, I zard un jist tha seam."

WIFE.

"Well Bob, ya bin an done it now,
A purty artvul trick I vow:
Var goodness seak dwoant let it out,
Ar vine neam we shood av about;
Var zartin zure, you an yer wife,
Hood be twitted we't ael our life.
I hopes till be a underd year
Vore nother Lection, we avs here."

MEAKEN OUT THA ZENSUS PEAPER.

HUSBAN TO WIFE.

"What's thic blue peaper there: top a teable?"

WIFE.

"A puzzler, Jarge: explain un I beant yeable;
Woold Vowler brought un in here tother day,
An zed nex Monday, he'd be vetch'd away.
When ax'd about it, he cut zich a keaper,
Drat tha ooman; tis tha Zensus Peaper.
Zensus, I zays: What, do em want ta rob
Poor voke a what leetle there's in their nob
A zart a grin'd, an zed twerden no joke;
King Edderd wants tha number of he's voke.
I zays, nuthen we hant yeard about it;
A zays, rade tha peaper if ya dout it.
An then a axed if arn a we cood write,
O eece, I zays, we can. Then thats ael right;

Structions be printed on tha peaper plain,
Zoo mine he's ready gean I caals again,
Var time da vlee, main ot I got ta do,
An mist be Monday night tha job get droo.
Right droo thease Parish a Langvird Steeple,
I've got to get tha number a tha people.

* * * * *

Ael right, I zays, Jarge ull sure ta do it,
When he've rade tha peaper, an zees droo it."

HUSBAN.

"Well, han tha peaper here, get pen an ink,
Let's vill un up, whiles on it I da think;
Var Monday marn I med be in a clit,
An goo ta wirk vargetten ael about it;
Var if teant done, gean Vowler he coms round.
I zees that thay can vine ess quite a pound.
Zoo stop the childern's prattle now a bit,
An roun tha kitchen teable ael o'ee zit.

* * * * *

Vust line: is var my neam; well, that's Jarge Brown,
Ael da know that, as lives in thease here town;
Next: Head of a vamly; a coose I be,
Ant I got a wife, an me childern dree?
Tha next is M, or F, ooman ar man,
A leetle question I dwoant unnerstan;
I aelwys thought a husban wur a man,
A wife a ooman, diden you, me Nan?
Cos it da zeem ta I mwoast martil quare,
To ax a zilly question like that are.

Next item, Age: well that I zoon ull do,
Vust a August las, I wur thirty two.
Then as to my perfession, ar me wirk,
A question too, I beant agwain ta shirk.
Fi'ather wur a Carter, an I'm a Carter too,
Var Varmer Vincin, as lives down Bell Vue.
Ta be a varmer's man yeant no disgrease:
Zom starchier voke av got a wusser pleace.
Wur wur I barn: why voke da knaa Jarge Brown,
Wur barn'd an bred in thease yer leetle town;
An wur I av a lived ael droo me life,
Christen'd, convirm'd, and married to a wife.
As to condition, dumb, zilly, ar blind,
Thank God, me zite is good, an zoos me mind;
Aelthough me wife zometimes caals I ninny,
An I she, at which boath oance da grinny;
I'm zoun in lim, nar beant gone off me hook,
Nar neet praps zich a vool as I da look;
Tho zometimes I'll own, when things gets out a rut,
A chap's clin'd ta think, a mist be off he's nut.

* * * *

Well now, I've vnish'd up thease yer vust line,
An what's put down is true, I'll swear, an zign.

* * * *

Now Missus, you comes nex; What's yer rite neam?
Anser vair an square, ya needen be a sheam."

WIFE.

"Why, Jarge! ya knows tis Frances Annie,
Tho zometimes I'm caaled Nan, an zometimes [Fanny."

HUSBAN.

" Frances Annie. Well, I've putt that down,
Male or female : well that tha lot da crown,
Ael as ever I did hear, ar ever zee ;
As tho a She cood be putt down as He.
Well, now yer age : now Nancy, tell it true,
When we wur married, you wur twenty-two ;
That's zix year agoo, if you remember,
Come tha twenty-haighth a nex Zeptember.
Zoo I'll putt it down here, ael vair and straight,
That Frances Annie Brown is twenty-haight."

WIFE.

" Now that's a fib, var zartin, Jargy Brown,
Zoo dwoant get putten zich a cracker down ;
I know, when we wur wed, I zed ta you,
I thought me age wur ard on twenty-two ;
Bit sister Zal, who's years woolder then I,
Zays she's bit twenty-zeven nex July.
Zoo if that's het, as true as I'm alive,
Las birthday I wur ony twenty-vive ;
Zoo putt that down, and dwoant bodder no mwore,
About my age, var that be right I'm zure."

HUSBAN.

" Now look here, Nan, I'll draa tha line an vix,
Yer age las birthday as jist tweny zix ;
I'm zure twunt never do var you to try,
An pass as zeven year younger than I.
Var tood be notic'd quick, an I'll be bound,
Var written fibs thay'd vine ess thic thar pound ;

As I zees be raden thay've power ta do.
If we da write down here what idden true.

* * * *

Now, Nancy, wur wur ee barn : zay me dear,
Ya av twould I, twur no where handy here;
What County wur't, Village, ar tha Town?
Cos it da zay it mist be ael putt down."

WIFE.

" Why shood em know, Jarge! what dicklus stuff:
Putt down Lunnen, thats plenty near anuff.
Zackly tha pleace: I cooden mine it now,
Bit twur zome peart a Lunnen, that I vow.
Var that's wur mother liv'd when I come down,
An took a pleace near thease yer leetle town,
As parlour maid, up there at Wincom Grove,
And were we I ya know ya vill in love."

HUSBAN.

" Eece, I'll put that down, till do main stunnen,
An let em zee me wife come vrim Lunnen;
Tho I be clined ta think 'tis ony fancy,
Var yer taak beant like a cockney, Nancy.
As ta condition, ya beant blind, nar diff,
Nar dumb I swear; not when we avs a miff.

* * * * * *

Zoo that da vinish up tha second line,
An ael I've put is true; I swear an zign.

Well, now about the childern, let me zee;
Two strappen bwoys, a beaby maid, that's dree;

Ther's Jack an Jim, now what's tha Beab ta be?
She hant bin neam'd ar christen'd heet ya zee.
We must put zummat, spoose we zay Fanny,
Ar atter you me dear, an neam her Annie."

WIFE.

"Begar, no Jarge; that shaant never be;
One neam's anuff in one vamily.
If she's neam'd Annie, till be auver town,
Which o'm de mane; woold Nance, ar young Nance [Brown;
Ower nayburs too, tid mainly bother,
To tell which vrim thic, ar thease vrim tother.
We'll av it Haignes, ar else Dorothy;
Tha last is a sweet purty name, ya zee."

HUSBAN.

"Eece, an thay'd caal her Doll ael droo her life;
No, no, we mussen av that ar me wife.
Now, what about Lizer, we caant beat that."

WIFE.

"Why, then thay'd call her Lize, ya zee girt vlat."

HUSBAN.

"Well, I spoose thay hood, now, what do ee zay?
Var ta av her neam'd and christen'd May.

WIFE.

Well I shood like that; look sharp, put it down,
Thay wunt be yeable ta nickneam "May Brown,"
Her age, zix weeks ony las Zadderdy;
Zoo mine tis zettled: Beaby's neam is May."

HUSBAN.

" Ael right, I very zoon ull putt that down,
May, the daater a Jarge an Annie Brown.

* * * * * *

" Well, now I've vinish'd up ; an every line
Is zartin true ; zoo here Jarge Brown I'll zign."

WIFE.

" Jist stop a minit, let I look it droo ;
Why tha bwoys age, ya av lave'd out that's true."

HUSBAN.

" An zoo I av ; Well, Jack a will be vive
In August nex, if then he be alive ;
Zoo, I mist putt un vawer, dwoant ee zee ;
An leetle Jimmy he is hard on dree,
Zoo I mist ony putt two year var he.
Nuthen's tha matter we narn o'ms noddle,
Main cute thay wur vore thay cood toddle.
Ther zites be good, thame zound in wind an lim,
Two strappen youngsters be our Jack and Jim."

* * * * * *

" Zoo now I think that's ael ther is ta do,
Bit praps you, Nan agean, had baste look droo."

WIFE.

" Eece Jarge I will ; well, purty rite da zeam,
Zoo now I thinks as you can zign yer neam."

HUSBAN.

" Gie me tha pen, an in me baste roun han,
I'll zign Jarge Brown in girt bwould letters gran ;
An let Vowler zee I be a schollard,
Aelthough tha plough I ael me life av voller'd ;
Zoo when a caals, a need'nt rant nar keaper,
Nar zay as ow we spwil'd tha Zensus Peaper."

THA OTTER HUNT.

Tis haight a'clock, a bright May marn,
An down tha vlow'ry mead ;
A crowd a voke, we yelpin hounds,
Be Nadders bainks is zeed.

Var marnen pray'r ; church bell da toll,
Tha dooer is aupen wide ;
Bit ony two'r dree totterin voke
Is zeed ta goo inzide.

Var tis tha annal Otter Hunt,
An za vine tha weather,
Spourtsmin, vrim town, an thay aroun
Be hurryen tagether.

Maing crazy-bets, and cuckoo vlowers,
An, maing dewy grasses ;
Come spourtsmin in ther jackets green,
Along we gaiter'd lasses.

Tha Cuckoo's ever welcome note,
Za mellar vills tha grove ;
An vrim yan copse, a Nightingale,
Za sweetly trills he's love.

Tha zun shines vrim a cloudless sky,
Zoft winds waffs gentle gales ;
Tha hounds begin ta snuff tha scent,
Their yelpen vills tha vales.

Tha Maaster blows he's zilver harn ;
Hounds, knaa tha welcome call,
An headlong in tha zilvery stream,
Tha laders rush asprawl.

Ael up an down, tha streamlet thay :
We hager eyes da look,
Thay poke their leetle noses in
Ta every leetle nook.

Tha brillent Kingvisher's loud wail,
Vloats on tha marnen air,
As maingst the willer roots, the hounds
Disturbs his pacevul lair.

An to an vro, on hache baink go,
Thase merry huntin voke ;
We poles, ta leap tha ditches wide,
An inta shallers poke.

On, on, thay go, we skip an jump
  O'er hedges, ditches, stiles.
Weout ado; tha lasses too;
  Beamin we artless smiles.

Tha vlooded mead, nooan o'm da mine,
  Nar muddied; nar wet veet,
Zich leetle things, thay trate we scarn,
  When Otter Hounds da meet.

Now to tha withy bade thame come;
  Ael hearts goo pit a pat,
A bwoy da swear: a Otters there,
  Zome zed, praps twur a rat.

A village yokel, looken on,
  Bawls out, "lar bless me zawl:
If I did'n zee a vurry thing
  Rin inta thic girt hawl."

An leetle Lucy, vows she zeed,
  A Otter near tha drawin;
Zoo huntsman puts tha hounds ta wirk
  A yelpen an a pawen.

He's hiden in tha trunk var zure.
  Tha hager spourtsmin cry;
If zoo; we zoon ull have un out,
  Ar knaa tha razon why.

Jack: bring tha leetle spanniel here;
  He'll zoon the trunk azend;
Now spourtsmin ael, look purty sharp.
  He'll bolt out tother end.

The leetle spanniel did bow wow,
  Ta scare poor leetle Otter,
An Jack, zoon at tha tother end,
  Zings out, begar I've got her.

We zitemint ael, turn'd var ta zee:
  Ther's no misteak in that,
There wur tho: var Jack in he's yarms,
  Held vast a *Tabby Cat.*

A roar a laffen then went up,
  Vrim thay as rin'd ta zee;
Poor puss wur vreed; an zoon wur perch'd,
  Up in a willer tree.

"Well! well"! zays ael tha spourtin voke;
  "Dear me," zays leetle Lucy,
"How coold I zoo mistaken be,
  Not ta know a pussy."

Her brother, he mist teak tha blame,
  Cos he hadden taught her;
To discern a Tabby Cat
  Vrim a river Otter.

Ael laff'd, but nooan look'd merrier,
  Then tha good woold Maaster,
Who wur za glad; Puss hadden met,
  We any cruel disaster.

Tha hounds look'd on, we tearvul eyes,
  Ael on em convounded;
Ta zee thic cat rin up tha tree,
  Thay look'd up astounded.

On topmwoast branch, we gleamin eyes;
  Puss watch'd tha dreaded voe,
Yelpen an racin vuriously,
  Aroun tha tree below.

Var Otter vlesh an blood thay wur
  Ael crazy to get at,
An velt disgusted when thay voun:
  Twur nuthen bit a cat.

The day wore on; no luck at ael,
  Thay cooden vine ther quarry;
Zoo hungry back ta kennels went,
  Tha hounds, looken main zorry.

Tha spourten men, an lasses too:
  No vurder keer'd ta roam,
Zoo gather'd up ther skirts an staves,
  An zoon mead tracks vor whoam.

An thus did end, thic Otter Hunt,
  In merrie month a May,
When Tom the drowners *Tabby Cat*
  Led ael tha vield astray.

* * * * * *

Now spourten voke, when next ya hunt
  Tha Nadders windin water;
Look up yer Nateril History,
  Ta tell ee Cat vrim Otter.

Bibliographical note

Slow's output is not easily catalogued. Many of his works were published anonymously, most are undated, although some have dated prefaces, some were issued or reissued in several forms, most carry two imprints, and there are minor discrepancies between covers and title pages. This list, which so far as is ascertainable is in chronological order of publication, is based on a list of thirty items appended to Slow's obituary notice in *Wiltshire Archaeological and Natural History Magazine*, vol. 43, 1927, pp.110–112, which I have corrected by inspecting all the items available in collections in Wiltshire, and to which I have added a number of other works. I have no confidence, however, that this list is complete, nor that it is completely accurate. I should be very interested to hear from any reader who possesses a Slow item not included in this bibliography.

1. Harvest home at Wilton. [1864]
[No copy available for inspection. Described in *Salisbury Times* 24.10.1913.]

2. Poems in the Wiltshire dialect: by the author of Harvest home at Wilton. Wilton: Alfred Chalke. London: E. W. Allen. 1867 [No copy available for inspection. Details from *W.A.M.* vol. 43.]

3. Voices from Salisbury plain: or Who's to blame? A dialogue on the Franco-Prussian war, between Willum and Jeames, (Wiltshire labourers.) by the author of Poems in the Wiltshire dialect. London: Simpkin, Marshall. Salisbury: F. A. Blake. [1870], 20p.
[Date supplied by newspaper cutting in Wilts. Cuttings,

16.147. Copy in W.A.S. Library, Devizes is bound with 5 below.]

4. The adventures of farmer John Bray, at the Wilton festivities, in honor of the coming of age of the Earl of Pembroke. [1870/1871], 26p. [Copy in W.A.S. Library, Devizes is bound with 5 below, lacking cover. A newspaper cutting in Wilts. Cuttings, 16.147 gives a date of 1871, but it must ante-date 5 below, which is dated 1870 in *W.A.M.* vol. 43.]

5. Rhymes of the Wiltshire peasantry, and other trifles, by Edward Slow, author of Who's to blame, John Bray, etc. etc. Salisbury: F. A Blake. Wilton: E. Slow, West End View. [1870/1871], iv, 122p. [See note to 4 above.]

6. Wiltshire rhymes: a series of poems in the Wiltshire dialect . . . never before published. London: Simpkin, Marshall. Salisbury: F. A. Blake. 1881, vii, 143p. [Swindon Local Studies Library has a copy printed "Second edition" on title page, but otherwise identical to other copies.]

7. The fourth series of Wiltshire rhymes by Edward Slow, Wilton, containing twenty-five new poems in the Wiltshire dialect, never before published, also a glossary of some words now used in Wiltshire and adjoining counties. Salisbury: F. A. Blake. Wilton: E. Slow, West End. 1889, 128p. [The glossary was expanded and issued separately. See 8 and 27 below.]

8. Glossary of Wiltshire words. Wilton: Wilton Printing Works [printer]. [1892], [12]p. [Also included in the 1892 edition of the Wilton almanac, according to a newspaper cutting in Wilts. Cuttings, 16.147. See also 7 above and 27 below.]

9. Tha parish council bill: a discussion twix Tom and Phil, two leabouren men. Reprinted from the Weekly Record. [1894] 4p. [Signed E.S.W. Date from manuscript note on copy in W.A.S. Library, Devizes. Subsequently included in 11 and 15 below.]

10. Smilin Jack: a true stowry of a midnight adventure. Wilton: Wilton Printing Works [printer]. [1894?], [6]p. [*W.A.M.* vol. 43 has date 1894?, but copy in W.A.S. Library, Devizes has manuscript note 1893?. Subsequently included in 11, 15 and 25 below, but the precise title varies.]

11. The fifth series of Wiltshire rhymes and tales in the Wiltshire dialect . . . never before published. Wilton: E. Slow, West End. Salisbury: R. R. Edwards. Gillingham: James Ridout. [1894], vii, 150p.

12. Bob Beaker's visit ta Lunnen ta zee tha Indian & Colonial exhibition. By the author of Wiltshire rhymes etc. Salisbury: R. R. Edwards. [1896], 18p. [Subsequently included in 17 below. *W.A.M.* vol. 43 has note, "A prose story prefixed to more than one local almanack for 1896".]

13. Original: Aunt Meary's soup—a true story. Salisbury: R. R. Edwards. [1896/1897], 4p. [Subsequently included in 17 below. Copy in W.A.S. Library, Devizes is bound in Edwards's Salisbury almanac compendium 1897.]

14. Ben Sloper's visit to the Zalsbury diamond jubilee zele-brayshun: what he zeed and zed about it. By the author of Wiltshire rhymes. Salisbury: R. R. Edwards. [1897], 19p. [Subsequently included in 17 below. *W.A.M.* vol. 43 has note, "Also prefixed to Edwards' Almanack for 1898".]

15. Wiltshire rhymes with glossary of over 1,000 words,

used by the peasantry in the neighbourhood of Salisbury by Edward Slow. Salisbury: R. R. Edwards. Wilton: E. Slow, West End. [1898/1900]. [Details from copies at Salisbury and Swindon Local Studies Libraries. Salisbury's copy has an autograph note, Sept. 1900. *W.A.M.* vol. 43 refers to, Wiltshire rhymes with glossary, new issue, 1898, 250p, and also cheap edition of 20 of the poems, 128p.]

16. Ben Sloper at tha military manoovers on Zalsbury plaain; being a humourous description of the various camps, battles, an tha girt march past (by the author of the Wiltshire rhymes and tales.). Salisbury: R. R. Edwards. [1898], 26p.

17. Humourous west countrie tales, by the author of Wiltshire rhymes. Salisbury: R. R. Edwards. [1899], 147p. [Includes items 12–14 above and extracts from 11 above.]

18. Ben Sloper an he's Nancy's visit to Barnum & Bailey's girtest show on earth at Zalsbury July 10th 1899: what thay zeed an zed about it, by the author of the Wiltshire rhymes and tales. Salisbury: R. R. Edwards. [1899], 23p. [Reprinted from the *Salisbury & Winchester Journal*, 1.7.1899.]

19. Zam & Zue's visit to tha "Girt Wheel". Salisbury: R. R. Edwards. [1900], 6p.

20. The Transvaal war: who's to blame? Boer or Briton: a dialogue between Willum & Edderd, two working men of Salisbury Plain, by the author of the Wiltshire rhymes and tales. Salisbury: R. R. Edwards. [1900], 26p.

21. Ben and Nancy Sloper's visit to Zalsbury Vair, what thay zeed and how thay enjoyed therzelves. Salisbury: R. R. Edwards. [1901], 30p.

22. Humourous west countrie rhymes, by E. Slow. Salisbury: R. R. Edwards. [1902], 36p. [Cover includes list of contents: Containing—Tha Wiltshire moonrakers, Tha puzzled voter, Meaken out tha zensus peaper, and an amusing prose sketch, entitled . . . Tha poachin case.]

23. West countrie tales: Ben & Nancy Sloper's good fortune: thier visit to Lunnen ta zee the Drury Lean pantomime of tha vorty thieves and to tha Allhamber Music Hall. Salisbury: R. R. Edwards. [1902], 31p. [This is presumably the work referred to in a newspaper cutting in Wilts. Cuttings, 16.147 as "Drury Lean Theayter".]

24. Chronology of Wilton, also an account of its bishops, abbesses, rectors, mayors, members of Parliament, churches, royal charters, hospitals, benefactors, celebrities, &c., compiled by Edward Slow. Wilton: Edward Slow. Salisbury: R. R. Edwards. [1903], 150p.

25. The Wiltshire moonrakers edition of west countrie rhymes. Salisbury: R. R. Edwards. London: Simpkin, Marshall, Hamilton, Kent & Co. [1903], 372p. [Also published in two volumes. This collection includes many poems from earlier volumes of rhymes, and some originally published as separate pamphlets.]

26. Buffalo Bill's wild waste show at Zalsbury, August tha zix, nineteen underd an dree by Janny Raa. Also a nigger dialogue, "the spider and the fly". Salisbury: R. R. Edwards. [1903], 20p.

27. Glossary of Wiltshire words compiled by E. Slow, author of the Wiltshire rhymes. Salisbury: R. R. Edwards. Wilton: E. Slow, West End. 1904, 15p. [See above, 8. This

edition exists in a copy bound with Dartnell and Goddard's *Wiltshire words* in W.A.S. Library, Devizes.]

28. Humourous west countrie tales, containing Tha bran figgetty pooden, . . . Salisbury: R. R. Edwards. [1903/1906], 39p. [Not included in *W.A.M.* vol. 43, and no copy in W.A.S. Library, Devizes. The work includes an advertisement for item 25 above (1903) and is referred to in 29 below (1906), but there is no more precise indication of date.]

29. Humourous west countrie tales,—no. 2. containing Tha pedigree vowls an tha Lunnen shearper . . . Salisbury: R. R. Edwards. [1906], 30p.

30. Tha military manoovers in tha nayberhood a Zalsbury Zeptember, 1907 by Measter Benjamin Sloper, being an account of the various operations, also the reception of the Wiltshire Regiment by the city of Salisbury. Salisbury: R. R. Edwards. [1907], 27p.

31. Reckerlections an yarns of a woold Zalsbury carrier var auver vifty years rote in tha Wiltshire dialect. Salisbury: R. R. Edwards. [1910], 61p.

32. The old age pension act: a dialogue between Fred, a woold varm leabourer and the squire's baillie: in the Wiltshire dialect. Also Good King Edderd's and Queen Alexander's visit ta Zalsbury an Wilton, June, Nineteen underd an haight. Salisbury: R. R. Edwards. [1911], 31p.

33. A humorous tale in the west countrie and cockney dialects entitled: Jan Ridley's new wife with an account of her London nephew Mister Dick Daisher. Salisbury: R. R.

Edwards. Wilton: Miss Winters and Wm. Jukes. [1913], 260p.

34. A leetle Willshere war ditty [signed Moonraker, E. S. Wilton]. 1917, 1p. [Poem on a single sheet, in Wilts. Cuttings, 15.132. Reprinted from *Wiltshire Gazette*, 29.3.1917.]

35. The great war: a west countrie dialogue between Fred & Mark, soldier & pacifist, by the author of Wiltshire rhymes & tales. Salisbury: R. R. Edwards. Wilton: Miss Winters. [1918], 26p.